High
School
Prodigies
Have It
Easy
Even in
Another
World!

2

Keine Kanzaki

DOCTOR

Introducing themselves as the Seven Luminaries and referring to Prince Akatsuki's magic tricks as divine miracles,

©Sacraneco

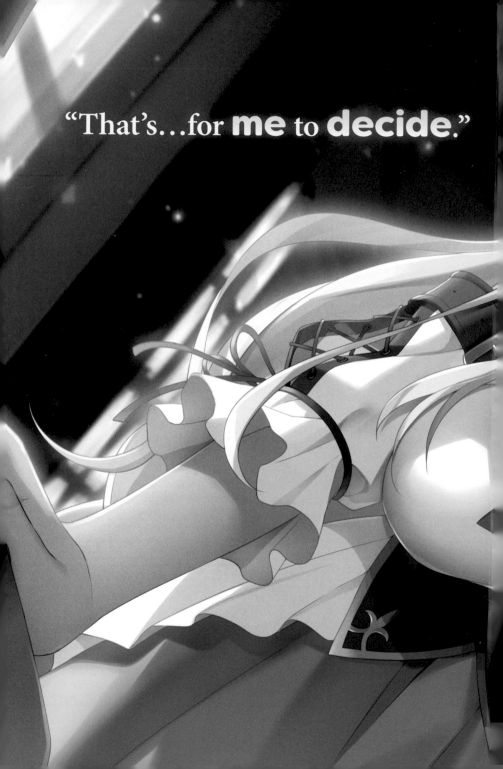

"That's...for **me** to **decide**."

Lyrule

©Sacranecc

Now then, what to do?

After being captured, Shinobu Sarutobi was stripped down to her underwear and chained to the wall by her wrists.

Shinobu
Sarutobi

JOURNALIST

©Sacraneco

CONTENTS

RIKU MISORA
ILLUSTRATION BY
SACRANECO

High School Prodigies Have It Easy Even in Another World!

High School Prodigies Have It Easy Even in Another World!

2

Riku Misora

Illustration by SACRANECO

YEN ON

NEW YORK

High School Prodigies Have It Easy Even in Another World! 2

Riku Misora

TRANSLATION BY NATHANIEL HIROSHI THRASHER
COVER ART BY SACRANECO

CHOUJIN KOUKOUSEI TACHI WA ISEKAI DEMO YOYU DE IKINUKU YOUDESU! vol. 2
Copyright © 2016 Riku Misora
Illustrations copyright © 2016 Sacraneco
All rights reserved.
Original Japanese edition published in 2016 by SB Creative Corp.
This English edition is published by arrangement with SB Creative Corp.,
Tokyo in care of Tuttle-Mori Agency, Inc., Tokyo.

English translation © 2020 by Yen Press, LLC

Yen On
150 West 30th Street, 19th Floor
New York, NY 10001

Visit us at yenpress.com
facebook.com/yenpress ★ twitter.com/yenpress
yenpress.tumblr.com ★ instagram.com/yenpress

First Yen On Edition: September 2020

Yen On is an imprint of Yen Press, LLC.
The Yen On name and logo are trademarks of Yen Press, LLC.

Library of Congress Cataloging-in-Publication Data
Names: Misora, Riku, author. | Sacraneco, illustrator. | Thrasher, Nathaniel Hiroshi, translator.
Title: High school prodigies have it easy even in another world! / Riku Misora ;
illustration by Sacraneco ; translation by Nathaniel Hiroshi Thrasher.
Other titles: Chōjin-Kokoseitachi wa Isekai demo Yoyu de Ikinuku Yōdesu! English
Identifiers: LCCN 2020016894 | ISBN 9781975309725 (v. 1 ; trade paperback) |
ISBN 9781975309749 (v. 2 ; trade paperback)
Subjects: CYAC: Fantasy. | Gifted persons—Fiction. | Imaginary places—Fiction | Magic—Fiction.
Classification: LCC PZ7.M6843377 Hi 2020 | DDC [Fic]—dc23
LC record available at https://lccn.loc.gov/2020016894

ISBNs: 978-1-9753-0974-9 (paperback)
978-1-9753-0975-6 (ebook)

1 3 5 7 9 10 8 6 4 2

LSC-C

Printed in the United States of America

⚜ Where Are the High School Prodigies? ⚜

A short time had passed since the plane carrying the famous Seven High School Prodigies vanished over the Pacific Ocean. Despite Japan losing its prime minister, the country remained surprisingly calm.

Thanks to how quickly Tsukasa Mikogami's Reformist Party had appointed an interim representative, turmoil and political stagnation were contained to a minimum.

The representative in question, Kenzo Ooiwa, had just returned home after pushing an agreement for which Tsukasa had laid the groundwork. It stipulated that Saudi Arabia would use Japanese companies in the construction of their underground maglev trains as well as other infrastructure projects.

"Good work today, Interim Prime Minister."

"You, too, Chang. You really saved my neck out there."

"Just doing my job, sir."

The trip had been long, and the schedule had been brutal. Ooiwa, who was in his sixties, was visibly exhausted. As he sat down at his desk, Chief Secretary Chang handed him a cup of slightly cooled tea.

"Something to drink, sir?"

"You're a lifesaver."

After grumbling about how long it had been since he'd had a proper break, the acting prime minister brought the cup to his mouth. A slight look of surprise crossed his face. Its flavor was entirely unlike the Japanese tea with which he was so familiar.

"It's sweet…almost soothing. What is this?"

"A tea made from red dates steeped in honey. They're so nutritious and so effective at relieving fatigue that we even have a saying about them back in my homeland: *yītiān chī sān zǎo, qīngchūn yǒng bùlǎo*—'three red dates a day make a man never age.'"

"I can see why. It's like they're filling my body with warmth and melting away all my weariness. This is nice." Ooiwa finished his tea, then took a short breather before speaking again. "So…what did the Fraternity Party get up to while I was away?"

"Much the same as always. They're trying to take advantage of the prime minister's absence to take the House of Representatives in the next election. They're calling for a dissolution nonstop. However, it doesn't appear their message is resonating with the voters. Refusing to demonstrate your own worth and just dragging others down to make yourself look better by comparison is a poor recipe for garnering support. Also, there's the whole situation with the DDSA's failed terrorist attack on your plane in Saudi Arabia. Thanks to the investigation into whether Fraternity Party Secretary-General Sugawara was the one who leaked them the flight plans, the group's split into the Sugawara faction, the Koizumi faction, and the Matsudaira faction. Their infighting isn't earning them any points, either."

"I see. Well, I hope their internal squabbling keeps them out of our hair for a while. We have enough trouble trying to fill Prime Minister Mikogami's shoes as it is."

After laughing wryly about how Tsukasa Mikogami did the work of ten people and made it look easy, Ooiwa turned his gaze back to Chang.

"Still, I want to thank you again for your work back there. If things had played out differently, I'd have been blown to smithereens over that desert... Honestly, I'm amazed you were able to figure out the connection between Sugawara and those terrorists. Even most of his own party members didn't know."

"I'm afraid I can't take much credit for that. The manual the prime minister left said to keep a close eye on Sugawara's movements. I was merely carrying out instructions."

"What an unbelievable document the *Three-Year Manual* is... It's the entire reason I was able to inherit this job so uneventfully."

The *Three-Year Manual*.

A document Tsukasa Mikogami had penned while he was in office. It had been written for use in the event that anything happened to him.

I'm not a prophet, so I can't predict the future with any certainty. However, there are a number of conjectures I can make based on the state of the world today.

As such, I've listed countermeasures herein to deal with any and all such events.

With that brief introduction, he went on to list five paths and a hundred end points the international community might reach over the next three years, as well as strategies to deal with various incidents that could occur along each branching route. The manual's existence was the sole reason the Reformist Party had been able to continue running the government so smoothly after Tsukasa went missing.

"Prime Minister Mikogami wanted to make sure that the country wouldn't descend into chaos if he were to ever be assassinated," Chang replied.

What was most shocking, though, was that the current state

of international affairs was laid out more or less to the letter under the incredible guidebook's "Root C3-1" section. When they'd seen that, the Diet's Reformist Party members had shuddered in fear and admiration at the sheer talent of the young man with whom they'd politically allied themselves.

"As a citizen of this nation, I have nothing but the utmost respect for him. What a truly astonishing individual."

"Because of his efforts, we should be fine for at least the next three years. I can only hope he returns before then."

For a moment, Ooiwa was at a loss for words. "'Return'? You still believe he's alive?"

"Of course." Chang's response was instant. "True, their beacon vanished over the Pacific. The natural conclusion would be that they crashed. But even after the protracted search we conducted with the United States, we didn't find so much as a scrap of metal from their plane. That means that there's no hard evidence to support the assumption they ever went down."

In other words, it was too early to give up hope.

"More importantly, Prime Minister Mikogami was the one who gave my life meaning and value after I lost not just my family but my very soul. He rescued me from being a mindless killer. Ever since then, my body and mind have existed solely to serve him. That's why I choose to believe that, someday, he'll come back… He's simply in the middle of something, and it's merely delaying his return."

CHAPTER 1

⚜ Obtaining the Dormundt City ⚜

After the septet of high schoolers with extraordinary abilities all vanished over the ocean, there was a good reason why the desperate search for them didn't turn up so much as a chunk of fuselage. They hadn't crashed in the sea. In fact, they'd landed in another world altogether. It was a world where knights and nobles prospered—like medieval Europe but with beastfolk and magic.

After crash-landing in the Freyjagard Empire, the High School Prodigies survived thanks to the help of the people of a village called Elm. Shortly after arriving in that unusual place, they immediately set out looking for a way to get back home. However, their efforts were interrupted.

A local lord, Findolph, kidnapped one of their saviors, a girl named Lyrule, and put the village to the torch. The people of Elm decided to fight back to stand up for their rights, fed up and furious over Findolph's corrupt governance. The Prodigies decided to lend them a hand. Together, they attacked the castle of the corrupt nobleman, took it over, and rescued Lyrule.

Yet the battle was far from over. How could it be? The empire wasn't going to forgive a group of commoners for baring their fangs at the ruling caste. It wasn't unlikely that an army was making its way toward the Findolph domain, ready to slaughter the people of Elm.

The villagers hoped to maintain their dignity—not as livestock to be spared or killed at the nobles' whims but as people with just as much right to exist as anyone else—after having revolted against the Freyjagard Empire. But was such a thing possible? Perhaps there was a way, though only one.

They had to establish a nation of the people, for the people, where social classes like nobles, commoners, and slaves were abolished and everyone was equal. In other words, a revolution was required. One that could spread the previously foreign values of liberty and equality for all throughout the land.

As it happened, the High School Prodigies were already taking the next step toward making that a reality. As for what that next step was—

"Hiiiiiyaaahh!!!!"

""""*Ahhhhhhhhhh!!!!*""""

The place: Ravale. A rural village in the Findolph domain with roughly a thousand residents. A rousing shout echoed through the air, followed shortly by the screams of a crowd.

The shout emanated from the swordmaster of the seven visitors from another world, Aoi Ichijou. The young woman was wearing a revealing leotard, fishnet stockings, and a bunny-ear headband.

The fear-laden screams, on the other hand, belonged to the people of Freyjagard, who were gathered around her. But why were they screaming?

The cause of the outcry could be found in the rectangular box sitting before the unusually dressed girl with the katana. A brilliant magician known as Prince Akatsuki was lying inside the container, his head sticking out one end and his ankles out the other. The onlookers had just watched in horror as Aoi had taken her katana and sliced through the box and Akatsuki's torso with it.

"No way! She really cut him in half?!"

"H-ha-ha, there's no way. If she had, it'd kill him..."

The throng of people was dotted with many pale faces. Master doctor Keine Kanzaki and the long-eared Lyrule, both of whom were wearing bunny outfits just as lascivious as Aoi's, wheeled each half of the box to the side to demonstrate that Akatsuki had well and truly been bisected. An even bigger cry issued from the crowd.

"Ahhh! Right down the middle?!?!"

"Eeeeek! Sh-she's a murderer!"

But the biggest surprise was yet to come.

"Bwa-ha-ha-ha! Fret not, fret not! I told you, didn't I?! I, Prince—or rather, God—Akatsuki, am a deity come down from the heavens in *hyuma* form! Being cloven in two is hardly enough to slay me!" Even though Akatsuki had been sliced in two and his top and bottom half were supposedly separated, he was still able to talk and wiggle his head and feet.

""""WHAAAAAAAAAT?!?!?!""""

The crowd was utterly stunned. Men and women of all ages shrieked, their eyes wide as dinner plates. Some of them even passed out from the shock of it all. Then, after Keine and Lyrule slid the box back together and unfastened the lock, Akatsuki sat up like nothing had happened and hopped from the would-be coffin in one piece.

"B-but how?! He should have been cut into pieces, yet now he's whole again?!"

"Impossible... What's going on...?"

The locals had no idea what to make of it.

Back on Earth, sawing a woman in half was a fairly standard

magic trick. Everyone knew there was some deception or contrivance behind it. But to the people of this world, who had little time for recreation and certainly hadn't heard of magic shows, it was downright astonishing.

A hushed whisper began traveling through the assembled onlookers.

"He's a god."

In Freyjagard, the emperor was the one and only absolute power. Something like a god simply wasn't allowed to exist. However, it was precisely because the concept was so harshly outlawed that the idea of an "all-powerful entity" had been passed down through the ages without fail. Could that really be what this blond kid was, though?

"Th-there's no way... It must just be magic or something..."

"No, that ain't it. I saw a few mages back when I was doing business in the capital, but I never heard nothin' about them being able to survive getting chopped in half...!"

"Yeah, that's right. Mages can talk to spirits, but other than that, their bodies are the same as anyone's. They can die by the sword like anyone else. And yet..."

"B-but there's no way he's really a god, right...?"

Akatsuki gazed out over the crowd from atop the large truck *slash* open-air stage Ringo Oohoshi, the Prodigies' own brilliant inventor, had built.

At best, the opinion of the crowd was mixed. That's why...

"Heh-heh. It sounds like we still have some skeptics in our midst! Very well! In that case...it appears I must show you a greater miracle! Turn that way and behold!"

As he shouted, he pointed toward the mountain resting under the western sky.

"That mountain's where our village is, but what about it...?"

"What's he—?"

As a bewildered stir started making its way through the crowd,

Akatsuki shouted "Boom!" and set off an explosion to obstruct the view of the great peak.

"Ahhh!"

"Wh-what's going on?!?!"

"There was an explosion all of a sudden, but…wait, huh? WHAAAAAAT?!?!"

Screams erupted from the people again. It was understandable. After all, when the explosion cleared…the mountain they'd been looking at just a moment ago was gone.

"Th-the mountain vanished?!?!"

"Ahhhhhhh!!!!"

"No, our village! How could he do such a thing?!"

"Worry not! Voilà!"

Akatsuki gave his fingers a loud snap.

The moment he did, a flash of white light appeared out of nowhere and momentarily blinded all who glimpsed it. As eyes adjusted and vision returned…

"You're kidding…"

"The mountain…the mountain is baaaaack?!?!"

"What? How? How can this be?!?!"

"See? Human magic like controlling wind and fire is but a parlor trick compared to my ability to reshape the very earth! *This* is the power of a god!" Akatsuki let out a loud laugh. The doubts that had been lingering in the throng's eyes were gone.

"Th-that's amazing…"

"He's the real deal… An actual god incarnate! There's no way a mere human could pull off something like that!"

Now they all believed the young blond. Every man and woman in that crowd was certain the boy was a god descended from the heavens in *hyuma* form. As Ringo Oohoshi looked out from behind the stage, she took her finger off the button that had triggered the flash of light.

"Akatsuki is...amazing," she said to Tsukasa Mikogami, the white-haired high school student *slash* prime minister beside her. Tsukasa nodded.

"That he is. The boy was made for the limelight. He's quite reliable in that respect," the politician whispered with satisfaction.

—Incidentally, what exactly were they all doing? Was this all just some normal magic show? Perish the thought. It had started the night the Prodigies claimed Marquis Findolph's castle.

That evening, after saving Lyrule and throwing a victory feast with the food they recovered from the lord's castle larders, the High School Prodigies waited for everyone else to fall asleep, then held a group meeting to plan their future steps.

"Now then, just as we discussed, we've successfully captured Lord Findolph and taken his castle. That said, we don't get to live happily ever after just yet." After Tsukasa spoke, genius businessman Masato Sanada nodded in agreement.

"Yeah, given where we're at, I'd say we're heading straight for happily *never* after."

"I concur. Even with us here, a single village has no hope of waging war against an entire nation," added Aoi.

"Precisely," Tsukasa affirmed. "So before the empire's main force arrives, we need to unify the Findolph domain."

"Didn't a bunch of soldiers make a run for it, though? Aren't they just gonna attack us from Dormundt?" Akatsuki's fears were well-founded.

However, Masato was quick to offer a rebuttal.

"Nah, I doubt it."

"Why?"

"Dormundt does have triple the soldiers this guy's castle did, but they're basically a glorified city watch. They don't have the training or the equipment to storm a fortified position like this. Plus, we captured their lord, so our opponents' hands are pretty much tied."

Tsukasa nodded in agreement. "Even if they did make a move, we're likely strong enough to fend off Dormundt's forces as is."

Simply put, such an eventuality wasn't one they needed to concern themselves with at the moment.

"What we *should* be worried about…is a unified, large-scale punitive incursion from outside the domain."

Depending on the scope of the army and the speed of their advance, there was a chance the High School Prodigies wouldn't be able to react in time.

Prodigious journalist Shinobu Sarutobi interjected with her thoughts on the matter.

"Actually, about that, we should be fine for a while."

"What makes you say that?"

"So between us and our neighbor, the Buchwald domain, there's this big mountain range called Le Luk, and apparently, it's real nasty up there. It's got these crossing wind spirit and water spirit ley lines or something. Basically, it has constant blizzards this time of year, and the temperature's always way below freezing. It's not some easy hike. Maybe experienced mountaineers could cross with light gear, but there's no way you're getting a full army with heavy armor and equipment and stuff through Le Luk during the winter. You'd end up going so slow that everyone'd just freeze to death."

"Oh right, now I remember. That fat-ass manager guy said something about going through Le Luk at this time of year being suicidal," remarked Masato.

"And they can't hit us by sea for a whole different reason," Shinobu added.

"Which is?"

"Right now, the Freyjagard Navy's busy trying to take over the place where Roo was born, the New World. Most of their warships are busy over there. They even sent boats from all the way up here in Findolph, so the southern ports probably look like ghost towns. There's no way they'll have the ships to mount a serious nautical offensive on us anytime soon. And if they only send a couple boats…"

"We can merely crush them one by one, that we can."

"Yeah, what Aoi said."

All in all, there was little concern that they'd have to face off against a proper army in the near future.

"I see," Tsukasa murmured after hearing Shinobu's theories. "You're right. It seems unlikely they'll be able to send a major force after us for a while. That should give us enough time to unite the Findolph domain under one banner."

"But how're we gonna do that, man?" asked Masato. "Our end goal's to make a nation where everyone is equal, but if we're trying to instill a noble cause in the masses, we can't exactly do that by putting the screws to 'em."

It was a task that required increasing their influence while simultaneously winning over the hearts and minds of the people. Such daunting prerequisites severely limited the group's options. When taking over a city like Dormundt, they couldn't just blast away the walls with a railgun cannon like they had Findolph's castle. If they invaded a city by force, its inhabitants would fear them, and terror bred hostility.

"…You got some sorta plan, Tsukasa?"

The prime minister gave his reply without hesitating for even a moment. He already knew exactly what would do the trick.

"As far as my plan goes… I think we should employ the power of religion."

"Religion? Really?"

"What? Why? We already took the castle—isn't that enough to start up a country? The goal is to set up a democracy, after all…" However, Akatsuki's question earned a headshake from Tsukasa.

"I'm afraid not. Even with democracy as our end goal, we can't just suddenly declare sovereignty and expect the people to follow us. The denizens of this world associate the concept of a *nation* with something that belongs to the privileged class—a concept that doesn't directly affect them. As far as they're concerned, it's none of their business. This creates a problem for us. We need them to want to join this revolution. A People's Revolution can't exist unless the common folk themselves believe they can change the world. And that's where religion comes in. A nation alone isn't enough to unify the will of a society. However, with a religion that espouses equality, we'll be able to work our way into their good graces. And thanks to Shinobu's intel, we know that the concepts of a *god* and *religion* have persisted despite the religious persecution here, so the idea should be easy enough for them to grasp."

"Oh yeah," Akatsuki remarked. "Now that you mention it, those soldiers did say something about 'swearing to God' when they were begging me for their lives…"

In other words, even if it was unclear if anyone actually still worshipped, the concept of a transcendental being was at least strong enough in people's minds for them to reference it.

"Furthermore, by using religion and introducing ourselves as a god and his attendants, we'll be able to set ourselves above humanity without having it contradict our message of equality. That represents a significant advantage to the tactic."

Masato gave Tsukasa's suggestion a big nod. "Oh yeah, that's a big one. Any time you form an organization, there's always gonna be people scrabbling for power within it. As this war heats up, we're gonna have to start flexing our strength more regularly. When that happens, we can't risk juggling any bullshit internal conflicts alongside it, but if we pretend not to be human from the get-go, that won't be as much of a problem."

"That's certainly true, but we also have to consider what will happen after all this is over and we return to Earth. If we led them as 'humans,' that could very well end up forming the basis of a new aristocracy, which would defeat the whole point. In order to give these people a smooth political transition once we leave, it's best if they don't consider us as simple mortals in the first place." Hearing Tsukasa's explanation, everyone let out little sighs of amazement.

"How very like you," remarked Keine. "You've already thought this all the way through to the end." Most of the other high schoolers were grateful that they had such a sagacious, reliable leader. However, Akatsuki still had doubts.

"B-but…there's no way it'll go that easily, will it? Getting them to fight the empire with us is one thing, but how in the world are we supposed to convince them that we're gods?"

Indeed, that was the big question. Between oppressive taxation, a cruel First Night Right system, and unjust laws that allowed nobles to kill commoners freely, the people were veritable powder kegs ready to explode on their rulers. However, unless the Prodigies convinced the masses that the seven of them were gods with the power to defeat the empire, they wouldn't be able to light the fuse.

Pulling something like that off was no small task. How were they going to convert the commoners into believers? Once again, Tsukasa responded without a moment's hesitation.

"It'll be easier said than done, but we have to show them a divine miracle impressive enough to take down the empire. That's where you come in, Prince Akatsuki…or rather, *God Akatsuki!*"

"Say what?" Akatsuki let out a baffled yelp at the unfamiliar moniker.

The other Prodigies were far less astonished, murmuring things like, "Oh, I get it" and "Ah, so that's the plan," with looks of understanding on their faces. Hearing them made Akatsuki go pale.

"Wait, wait, hold up a minute. I've got a really bad feeling about this. You don't mean..."

"I do indeed. I'm glad you're so quick on the uptake. Starting tomorrow, you'll play the part of a living god and win the people over with magic shows."

"WHAAAAAAAAAAT?!?!"

"Yo, Prince, pipe down."

"I—I—I—I—I will do no such thing! I'm a magician, remember?! I'm no god! I can't perform miracles! All my magic relies on illusion, I'll have you know...!"

"Though the idol will be false, their faith will be real."

"What are you, some sort of cult leader?!?!" As Akatsuki loudly protested the role he'd been given, an enthused Shinobu offered her own take.

"Oh, hey! If Akatsuki's God, does that make us his angels?"

"Something to that effect, yes," replied Tsukasa. "I don't know if they'll be familiar with the concept, but as previously established, we want to avoid referring to ourselves as human."

Masato agreed. "Hey, I'm down. Religion was a big driver in the Yellow Turban Rebellion, and that was the biggest peasant revolt in Chinese history. If Earth history as a whole is anything to go off, war and religion go together quite well."

"I see no reason to object, either," added Keine.

"Nor do I," Aoi said.

"Mmm..." Ringo Oohoshi, genius inventor, nodded in agreement as well.

Everyone turned toward Akatsuki. He shrank back a bit under the weight of their united gaze.

"...I-is this really happening?"

©Sacraneco

"Akatsuki." Tsukasa placed his hand on the magician's shoulder and looked the young man in the eye while he spoke. "This is an important job, and you're the only one who can do it. Can I count on you?"

"Unh…" As the mismatched red and blue eyes bore into him, Akatsuki let out a weak little groan. Eventually, though, he exhaled a breath he'd been holding and voiced his consent.

"All right, all right, I'll do it. I mean, it really does sound like I'm the only one who can… There aren't any large-scale, godlike magic tricks I can pull off on my own, though, so I'll need some help."

"Of course," promised Tsukasa. "I certainly didn't intend to have you shoulder the task alone."

Shinobu then suddenly moved to offer a question. "By the way, Tsukes, do you have a name for our religion yet?"

Tsukasa nodded as he gave his reply.

"We're going to call ourselves the Seven Luminaries."

The others responded with looks of amazement. It was an almost astoundingly obvious choice. If they operated under that name, there was a chance they could draw people who knew about the original Seven Luminaries out of the woodwork. That way, they'd kill two birds with one stone—organizing their revolt while simultaneously looking for information on how to get back home.

"Ooh, clever. You never miss a beat, do you?"

Tsukasa responded to Shinobu's praise with a small shrug. "I wouldn't be very good at my job if I did. Now then…in order to make this Seven Luminaries thing work, I have jobs I'll need each of you to carry out."

The prime minister's eyes scanned the assembled High School Prodigies.

"Akatsuki, you're up first. Like I just said, you're going to be traveling around Findolph and using your magic to win the support of the people. Next up, Ringo."

"...!"

"I want you to build him a means of transportation. I was thinking a large truck that could double as a stage… Can you make it happen?"

With a troubled look on her face, Ringo whispered her answer in his ear.

"I, um, I don't think we have enough iron and copper…"

"What if you melted down the castle's fences and extra equipment from its armory?"

"Oh…" The prodigious inventor hadn't thought of that. The girl was far too reserved for her mind to immediately leap to brazenly taking other people's property. Thus, Tsukasa's comment had come as a shock at first, but Ringo quickly changed her tone.

"That should work. I can draw its power from Bearabbit's battery, so…yeah, I can have it up and running in the next two days."

"In that case, we should bring the materials over to your workshop in Elm. Now then, Aoi and Keine. I want you two to accompany Akatsuki on the truck, driving off bandits and healing the sick 'in the name of the Seven Luminaries.'"

"Hee-hee," Keine giggled. "So you would have us win them over through philanthropy?"

"That's certainly part of it, but the fact also remains that we toppled the local government when we took over the lord's castle. Even if he wasn't doing his job, that doesn't mean we can slack off, too."

"Very well, then."

"You can count on us, that you can!"

After getting Keine's and Aoi's approval, Tsukasa turned next toward the resident ninja-journalist.

"As for you, Shinobu, I want you to cross the Le Luk Mountain Range and sneak into the Buchwald domain. From there, you can keep an eye on the empire's movements."

"Ooh, spy work."

"As rough as the mountains are, I doubt they'll pose much of a problem for you."

"Sha-sha! Easy-peasy! If I can smuggle myself onto Air Force One, I can get myself across a few mountains."

"I would ask that you try to avoid causing any international scandals, but…I trust your judgment."

"Oh, but if I'm gonna try and cover all that ground, I'd like a partner. Ideally someone nimble so they don't slow me down."

"What about Elch?" Masato suggested. "The guy's got a decent head on his shoulders, and his stamina won't be a problem, either."

"Oh yeah, El-El sounds perfect."

"In that case, I'll go ask him myself. Now, lastly, we have Merchant. I need you to head to Dormundt immediately and start spreading pro–Seven Luminaries propaganda."

"So all I gotta do is get them to like us? Easy."

"…Once the soldiers who fled there from the castle tell the mayor what happened here, he's likely to come down hard on the Elm Trading Company. He might even seal the gates, fearing we'll attack the city. The situation is dangerous, which is why you're the only one who can pull this off. What do you say?"

Masato replied with a nod and a loud, unconcerned laugh. "Consider it done. Unlike last time, I've got money to burn now. As long as I've got capital, I can do anything. When I'm done with 'em, they'll be begging to have the Seven Luminaries in their lives."

Masato wasn't the type to start things he couldn't finish. Tsukasa had been around him since elementary school, so he knew that full well.

That long relationship was why the prime minister merely replied with "Good" before addressing his fellow Prodigies as a whole.

"Now then, ladies and gentlemen, let's go make history."

And thus, having decided to use religion to engender the people's trust, the High School Prodigies traveled across the Findolph domain. They worked to earn the faith and devotion of its citizenry with Akatsuki's magic, Keine's medicine, and Aoi's contributions to public order. Villages began crowding under the Seven Luminaries' umbrella one after another.

As more settlements came into the fold, rumors about this new faith spread like wildfire. Even people from other villages started hurrying to nearby communities to catch the magic shows. Altogether, the audience in Ravale swelled to nearly five thousand attendees.

Akatsuki stood before the crowd. "Set your hearts at ease, my good people! We didn't descend upon this land to subjugate and rule over you! No, we came to reject the unjust nobles who use meaningless things like bloodlines as pretexts to tyrannize and persecute their fellows! We came to build a world where all can live together as equals!" The young magician laid out the Seven Luminaries' dogma while yanking the sheet off a rectangular object sitting on the corner of the stage.

Beneath the cloth rested a cage. Confined within, bound and gagged, was the man the Prodigies and the people of Elm had captured when they'd stormed the castle the other day—Marquis Findolph.

"Who's the fatty?"

"Given his physique, maybe a noble?"

Most responded to the sight of their former ruler with a resounding bit of confusion as to his identity. Such a reaction was expected, however. This world didn't exactly have photography. Most people had never seen Edwart von Findolph before.

There were exceptions, however…the young women.

"Wait, that's…!"

"I'd recognize him anywhere! That's Marquis Findolph!"

The moment they saw his face, their expressions flared with rage. All of them were victims of the inhumane First Night Right. None among them would soon forget the nightmare of having a hideous man they didn't love run his tongue over their bodies during one of the most emotional periods in their lives.

Many of the poor ladies suffered severe mental trauma, and some had even developed such strong aversions to physical intimacy that they ended up breaking off their engagements. Anger quickly spread among the men as well.

"That bastard!"

"So wait, that's the creep who took my daughter and…!"

Even though they hadn't suffered any harm personally, the creature in the cage had been the one who'd violated their beloved wives and daughters. The hatred of the crowd knew no bounds. The ferocious bloodlust emanating from the spectators was so intense that the confined Findolph soiled himself.

Seeing the pathetic man forced the mass of onlookers to realize something. The rumors they'd heard about how the Seven Luminaries were occupying the lord's castle were all true.

As they began to accept that, a thought began creeping through the hearts and minds of the common people. They started to believe that perhaps these extraordinary deities really could build a world with no nobles or commoners, just people living as equals. Some began shouting questions from the crowd.

"So if we follow you, the nobles won't be able to have their way with us anymore?!"

"Absolutely!"

"We'll be able to live better lives?"

"Absolutely!"

"And you can even cure my hemorrhoids?!"

"Uh…absolutely!"

Akatsuki answered all their questions in the affirmative, then floated up in the air and addressed them with a loud cry.

"As long as you believe in me and my attendants, then I swear to you here and now that once we see this holy war through, a future awaits you where none will be persecuted for foolish reasons like the circumstances of their birth!

"But never forget! The battle is yours to wage! We aren't here to just swoop in and save you. That would make us the same as your oppressors! How would that be any different?! If you want change, if you want to make change possible, each of you needs to declare independence and take up the fight yourselves!

"If you can muster the courage to do that, we will surely lead you to victory! Now, let's take those knights, those nobles, and their emperor, and smash their unjust rules to pieces! It's time to show the world that the future doesn't belong to them! It belongs to each and every one of you!"

Hearing such a provocative statement, the crowd took a moment to catch their breath, closed their eyes, and eventually—steeled their resolve.

"Let's do this! I'm in!"

"Yeah, me too! I never want my daughter to have to go through what I did!"

"He's right! This is all kinds of messed up! Why should the nobles get to live the good life in the cities while we have to toil in the mud from dawn to dusk?! That shit ain't right!"

Before long, their roars drowned out all else. Tsukasa gazed out at his friends with a satisfied look on his face. "He may have been reluctant at first, but once he got up on that stage, Akatsuki was a consummate professional. I have to say, he's a master at working a crowd."

"That…that makes pretty much all the rural villages now, right…?"

"It does. And we've successfully converted them all to following the Seven Luminaries. What remains is how we're going to deal with Dormundt and the nobles therein, but—"

No sooner had Tsukasa mentioned it than his phone rang. He was getting a call from the guy who'd sneaked into Dormundt and was currently spreading propaganda for their new religion.

"Hello?"

"Yo, man. Been a couple days now."

"Everything going okay, Merchant?"

"What, are you worried about me or something?"

"We heard word that Dormundt closed all its gates and has been on high alert. You didn't get attacked or anything, did you?"

"Ha! Compared to getting investigated by the National Tax Agency, things here have been a breeze. I'm just calling to let you know that the iron's hot right now. People all over town are begging to see the Seven Luminaries."

"Oh?" replied Tsukasa in surprise. "Well, that was quick. What on earth did you do to those people?"

"Who, me? I just handed out some blessings from God, that's all."

"Ahhh! Open the gates, open the gates! Please, I need to go buy mayo from the Seven Luminaries!"

"Oh no, the mayo… It's all gone… I feel like I'm gonna die…"

"*I'll believe in God! I'll believe in anything! Just gimme that mayonnaise!*"

"…"

"*See? And it's like that everywhere, by the way. Honestly, they're on the verge of rioting.*"

"…I see. I think I have a grasp on the situation now, thank you."

Historically, people had started wars over pepper and black tea. In other words, rioting over mayonnaise was certainly plausible. Outlandish, maybe, but plausible. Reasonably satisfied, Tsukasa gave Masato his new instructions.

"Nice work. That should be good as far as PR activities go. For now, I need you to lie low until I can set my plan into motion. In fact, let me reiterate: *Don't do anything.* Is that clear?"

"*So about that, you're probably gonna wanna act sooner rather than later.*"

"Why's that?"

"*A little bird told me the mayor's been hiring a lot of sailors.*"

"…Hmm. That means he's planning on abandoning the city and fleeing."

Such a development posed an issue. The position of a mayor meant his opinions had the power to unify all of Dormundt. Without him, the city would descend into chaos. As far as Tsukasa was concerned, the cleanest solution would be to bring the city and its mayor over to his camp in one fell swoop.

Now that seemed difficult. What was the best way to handle this?

"I'll have to think about that, so I'm going to hang up to preserve battery. I'll contact you in a bit with more instructions. For now, just hang tight." With that, Tsukasa ended the call.

Right as he did, Akatsuki hopped down from the stage. Behind it, where the audience couldn't see him, the magician threw off his cloak and plopped down onto the ground.

"Man, I'm beat. I've never had to work back-to-back-to-back like that before."

Tsukasa handed the blond boy a wooden cup full of tea.

"You did good work up there, Akatsuki. With your efforts, we were able to sink the Seven Luminaries' roots down all across the domain. Also…I just got a call from Dormundt. It sounds like we're quite popular over there, too."

"Wait, already? Man, Masato works fast."

Akatsuki gulped down the tea, visibly impressed.

"Apparently, he got them all addicted to mayo."

The blond magician gave a magnificent spit-take.

"Pfft! Gack! A-addicted to mayo?! Can that even happen?!"

"He said he was handing it out as a blessing from God. You know, like manna."

"*How is that like manna?!* You owe Christianity and Judaism an apology! Besides, what kind of messed-up God spreads something that sticky from the heavens?! Is that gonna be my divine legacy?!"

"It's only a difference of a few letters between mayonnaise and manna; don't worry about it." Tsukasa responded to Akatsuki's complaints halfheartedly but quickly offered his sincere gratitude. "In any case, you really did do well. It's thanks to you that we were able to establish the Seven Luminaries so successfully. It's good to have you on our side."

"Aw…" The blond performer scratched his cheek in embarrassment. However, he wasn't the only one who'd been working hard.

Ringo had built the truck and stage. Lyrule and Aoi had helped with the show. Keine had even used her medicine to win over the people's hearts in tandem. It had truly been a team effort.

And that being the case, now it's time for me to pull my weight, thought Tsukasa. He pulled out his phone and sent a text.

We're heading your way tonight. Let me know how you want to rendezvous.

Dormundt, the largest metropolis in the Findolph domain, had all its gates sealed and was on high alert. Soldiers who'd fled Findolph's castle spread the word that people from Elm—who were now calling themselves "the Seven Luminaries"—had taken the keep and captured its lord. However, the city's precautions were quickly proven fruitless.

Immediately after the Prodigies held their strategy meeting, Masato and Roo had taken a horse toward Dormundt, used a set of armor they'd recovered from the battle to impersonate a Bronze Knight and his slave, joined the soldiers fleeing the castle, and infiltrated the city. Once inside, the two started pulling strings and spreading rumors about the Seven Luminaries.

"I heard that a god and his attendants descended from the heavens to spread a message of equality."

"Someone said they can cure any disease."

"Word is, that 'mayonnaise' stuff Elm Trading Company used to sell was actually a divine blessing from the Seven Luminaries."

Some folk hated the nobles. Others were grief-stricken over ill family members. More just couldn't forget that wondrous flavor. Regardless, as the rumors continued making the rounds through the streets, the clamoring for the Seven Luminaries began to grow. Such longing quickly turned to hostility toward the mayor and his guards—the ones keeping the city on lockdown.

The people's increased anger toward the nobles forged a vicious cycle, and before long, riots broke out across the city. Dormundt had never seen such unrest. Its mayor, Count Heiseraat, had responded to the crisis by taking all the nobles who lived in the High-End Residential District and sheltering them in his mansion.

Dormundt was the only metropolis in the domain. There were all sorts of diversions and amusements that could only be found there. As a result, even the barons and other nobles entrusted with managing smaller cities and collecting taxes called it home most of the year. However, the high concentration of affluent households meant there simply wasn't enough personnel to protect them all.

When Heiseraat made his decision, the nobles were quick to gather at his estate. They'd heard the people's cries for equality growing louder by the day. They recognized the danger they faced. Once all the wealthy had taken refuge, they spent their days partying and drinking away their troubles.

"What's with all this 'equality' rubbish?! Those filthy peasants are getting too full of themselves!"

"I really must agree. We're nobles who serve the emperor, and they're little more than wild beasts. Calling the two equal is base foolery."

"Count Heiseraat, you need to put that rabble in its place!"

"Well said! It's absurd we can't peacefully venture outside. What does the city watch think they're doing?!"

Complaints raining on him from all sides, Count Heiseraat sighed. "As per the orders of the captain of the guard, Silver Knight Zest du Bernard, they're doing the best they can to keep things in check. There just aren't enough guardsmen to quell with these constant riots. That's why we haven't been able to track down the mayonnaise smugglers or Elm personnel, either."

In other words, things were getting worse, not better, for the nobles. The assembled wealthy, their faces flush from the alcohol, reacted to Heiseraat's explanation with indignant shouts.

"You're being too soft on them, Mayor!"

"Baron Clive is right! All you've done to the rioters and agitators is detain them! That's no way to get those ruffians to stay in line!"

"Yeah! You should take the rioters and their families, hoist them on pikes, and line them up in the central plaza for everyone to see! The only way to shut those peasants up is through fear!"

"…I will strongly consider such suggestions." Audibly drained, the count rose from his seat and turned to leave the banquet hall.

"Yeah, you do that!"

"You know, I've been worried about how soft you've been for a while now, Count Heiseraat. It was only a matter of time until something like this happened!"

"It really was. Lord Findolph put me in charge of Ravale, and let me tell you, I run a tight ship. When I get back, I'll force the commoners to prostrate themselves naked on the regular so I can drum those insipid ideas about equality out of their heads."

"Oh, what a wonderful idea. Words never get through to people like them, after all. In the village my husband runs, he takes the family with the worst harvest each year and burns their children at the stake. Why, it's simply hilarious how hard they all work now. When it comes to savage beasts, you have to beat the manners into them."

"Yeah, yeah! After all—"

As Heiseraat passed through the door leading from the banquet hall to the hallway, the voices of the incensed nobles grew distant.

"…What a bunch of carefree fools." The mayor's words were harsh. It was an understandable sentiment, however, considering the party in question busied themselves by getting drunk in his banquet hall.

None of them believed. Not one of them had accepted the reality that the lord's castle had fallen and that they were all alone in the remote north. Instead, they all trusted that they'd be able to keep living the same lavish lifestyles they always had.

But who could blame them?

The Findolph domain was so isolated that it hadn't seen war since the land was first cultivated. Such peace was why the concept of conflict was so foreign to them. It had blinded them to the ruin they were headed for that was sure to be unlike anything anyone holed up in the manor had ever seen.

In fact, Heiseraat himself hadn't believed it until he'd sent a scouting party to check what state the castle was in.

Now that I think about it, though, I shouldn't be surprised that a group who could make something so fine could pull something like that off.

Heiseraat glanced at the gold watch hanging around his wrist.

He'd received it as a gift from Masato of the Elm Trading Company in exchange for a license to do business in the city. The little accessory's construction was so delicate, it seemed nigh otherworldly. The fact that people with the scientific prowess to build its like could also blow up a castle wall was simply a matter of course. Considering this, the count realized something else, as well.

We're only alive because our enemy allows it.

If the Seven Luminaries were so inclined, they could engulf Dormundt in flames before lunch. There was no guarantee that he and the other nobles would still be alive this time tomorrow.

Using the manner in which the empire treated the people it subjugated as a benchmark, they'd be lucky to be forced into slavery. Heiseraat couldn't bear to suffer such a thing. He needed to take the nobles and flee Dormundt as quickly as possible.

I already have a ship ready in the port…

It was a small sailboat designed for fishing.

He was going to load it up with as many riches as it could hold, then leave Dormundt before daybreak.

And in order to do that, I'll need to turn in early!

The count mulled over his plan again and again as he opened the door to his bedchambers. Inside, he found a maid in the middle of making his bed. As the mayor was retiring unusually early, she hadn't finished her job in time. Heiseraat clicked his tongue and entered the chamber.

"Whatever, it's fine as it is! Just get out already! I have an early start tomorrow!" Shouting at the maid, he headed across the room and snuffed out its candle.

There came the sound of a door clicking shut. The maid must have left. However, when Heiseraat turned around to head toward the bed...he saw the maid standing before the closed door.

"What do you think you're doing? I told you to—"

"You've got an early start tomorrow? Going somewhere, are we?"

"Wha...?!"

A pair of eyes, one frigid blue and the other burning red, glinted at the startled nobleman through the darkness. The voice was clearly youthful, but it had an unmistakable gravity nonetheless. Heiseraat realized immediately this wasn't his maid.

"Damn you!"

"Don't move."

"Wh—!"

His intuition had been on the mark.

The maid—or rather, Tsukasa Mikogami wearing a maid uniform—withdrew a pistol from his apron and leveled its barrel at the count.

That shape, that's a—

"You're an erudite man, Count Heiseraat, so I'm sure you know what this is."

"...A gun. And one small enough to hide in a pocket! You have access to the imperial workshops' finest technology?!"

"I'm glad we're on the same page. Now have a seat in that chair there. Once you do, I'll lower my weapon."

"…"

"All the way down, if you don't mind."

"A-all right, all right…"

Heiseraat had been perched on the edge of the chair but did as instructed, sinking backward. When he complied, Tsukasa finally lowered his gun.

"I apologize for my crude behavior. I wanted to have a conversation with you without anyone else butting in, you see." Then, with a slight bow, the young man with the gun politely introduced himself.

"I'm one of the angels who serves Akatsuki, the God of the Seven Luminaries. I go by the name Tsukasa Mikogami."

"And you're here to kill me?" Fear resonated in Heiseraat's voice, but Tsukasa shook his head.

"Not in the slightest. I came as a representative to clear up some misconceptions you seem to have."

"Misconceptions…?"

"Precisely. You sealed all the gates, cowering from us as if we were invading barbarians, and you were even prepared to sacrifice the city to escape. But none of that was necessary. We of the Seven Luminaries aim to correct inequality, but that doesn't mean persecuting the nobility.

"We'll obviously have to reprimand any nobles who committed acts of cruelty against the people, but…we certainly have no intention of seizing your lives or your property. In fact, I had hoped you all might cooperate with us."

"How so…?" asked the count.

"Intelligentsia are scarce in this world. There are things only you can do. We would have you continue in your duties.

©sacraneco

"You will, of course, be compensated. If you flee, you'd spend the rest of your life in a foreign land, eating through the paltry riches you manage to take with you while constantly having to keep one eye out for the empire while watching for us with the other. But if you stay, I can guarantee you'll at least be comfortable. So..."

Tsukasa punctuated his words with a brief silence before going in for the finish.

"...as mayor of Dormundt, will you pledge allegiance to us?"

He was promising to treat Heiseraat fairly. Yet, even so, the count refused to let his guard down. "...You're the traitors who overthrew our ruling lord. Why should I trust you?"

Tsukasa tilted his head to the side, not quite following.

"Why should you not? Think about it for a moment. We blew through the castle's fortified walls. We can make mountains vanish. We can appear undetected in your bedchamber. With one squeeze of my finger, I could end your life right here and now. So why haven't I? The answer is simple. We don't seek needless bloodshed."

"And...if I still refuse?"

"If you're that determined to shackle your fate to that of a doomed empire, I won't stop you. The blood of you and your ilk will serve to wash away the old era. This is a war, after all."

"...!" Deep in Heiseraat's heart, he trembled. It was that eye.

The moment Tsukasa answered Heiseraat's question, his blue eye's glint had felt like a cold knife against the mayor's throat. That quiet power of Tsukasa's had demonstrated something to the count. If push came to shove, the young man before him wouldn't hesitate to kill.

After all, Tsukasa understood. He understood what it meant to reshape the times. The only thing that could wash away the old era was the blood of those who'd benefited from it.

He has me...utterly beat.

In fact, their defeat had been sealed the moment the castle had been seized. Still sitting, Heiseraat hung his head and acquiesced. "All right, you win. Dormundt hereby pledges loyalty to the Seven Luminaries."

"Thank you for being so understanding."

"But know this—the empire is formidable. Especially the Warden of the North, the one they call the Fastidious Duke, Oslo el Gustav. Unlike me, that man won't submit to words alone. He'll fight you to the bitter end, even if every ally he has falls."

"Do you still think you can prevail?" Heiseraat asked. Perhaps it was his final act of obstinacy as a noble. However, Tsukasa immediately replied with a faint smile playing at his lips.

"I see. Well, when that happens, we'll be sure to call on you and your friends for help."

"..." When he saw the amiable look in Tsukasa's eyes, the mayor found himself speechless for a moment. It really did seem like this young man was planning on relying on the nobles for aid at some point. That was when the count realized just how serious this Tsukasa was.

Instead of just wiping out the wealthy, he really was asking for their help building a world with no nobles or commoners. He wasn't using sophistry to manipulate the common folk. He was speaking from the heart.

Was such a thing even possible? Heiseraat had no idea; the man couldn't even begin to imagine it. However, he could tell this white-haired youth saw such a future with perfect clarity. That, if nothing else, the mayor was certain of. Knowing that sparked his curiosity far more than even the wristwatch had.

"Heh-heh, ah-ha-ha-ha! Very well then, Mr. Tsukasa! I look forward to seeing this world you envision!"

So it was that Mayor Heiseraat swore allegiance to the Seven

Luminaries. Tsukasa and the others had gained complete control over the Findolph domain.

The next day, Count Heiseraat opened the gates and personally announced to the people that he was handing sovereignty of the city over to the Seven Luminaries.

Thanks to the groundwork Masato had laid, the vast majority of the populace reacted to the news favorably, and on that day, there was a festival all throughout Dormundt. The Seven Luminaries even provided high-grade meat, fruit, and alcohol taken from the stores of Findolph's castle. Though the sun was high in the sky, everyone in the city was drinking, eating, and dancing.

Noise and excitement filled the air. A short distance from the bulk of the crowd, the High School Prodigies were gathered, laughing about something.

"Ah-ha-ha-ha! Check out how great it looks on him!"

"Right?! It's almost unsettling how well it suits him!"

They had all crowded around to see the picture Masato was displaying on his smartphone. On the screen was a picture of Tsukasa in his maid uniform from when he'd stolen into the mayor's mansion the day before.

"I'm telling you, back when I bribed the actual maid and had him change into her uniform, I was stifling so much laughter, I thought my head was gonna burst!" chuckled Masato.

"Oh? But he looks ever so adorable. Doesn't he just, Aoi?" asked Keine.

"Wh-why yes, that he does. And besides, wearing women's clothing was necessary for him to perform his mission, so it hardly seems polite to laugh at him for—"

"I got a low-angle shot, too."

"Snrk!" Unable to hold it in any longer, Aoi let out a giggle.

"Hwah!" For some reason, blood began gushing from Ringo's nose.

"Whoa, Ringo, you okay?!" Worried, Masato offered her a handkerchief, but instead, she grabbed his arm.

"Uh, um, I—can I...!" The inventor's face went bright red as she desperately tried to ask him for something. Seeing the desire in her eyes, Masato gave her a devilish grin.

"Oh, I get it. Don't worry, I gotcha. I'll send you the pictures later."

"Thank...you...!"

"...If you're enjoying yourselves that much, then I suppose it was all worth it." Tsukasa sighed as he watched the others getting ecstatic over the images. "We really do need to get to business, though. I didn't ask our friends from Elm to clear the area just so we could sit around and gossip."

"Y-yeah, yeah, I know," said Akatsuki. "Still, you gotta admit it was pretty funny."

"Oh, for sure," added Masato. "And you're up next, Prince!"

"Wait, why me?!"

"It's kinda your thing, isn't it? If you're not careful, Tsukasa's gonna steal your shtick right out from under you!"

"If that's my shtick, he can have it!"

Keine cut them off. "All right, you two, that's quite enough of that... So, Tsukasa, what exactly would you have us do next? It would appear that our initial objective—unifying Findolph—is more or less complete."

"Take the initiative and strike the other domains, is it?"

Tsukasa shook his head at Aoi's question. "We need to learn more about our opponents before we engage in any major military action. If nothing else, I want to wait until we hear back from Shinobu once she and Elch infiltrate Buchwald. For now, we should prioritize domestic affairs and solidify our foothold here.

"We'll need to overhaul the tax system, sort out the chain of command, and put together a legal code. Our end goal is to establish a nation, and doing so will require mountains of work. That said, most of that will fall on my shoulders. As for the rest of you…"

Tsukasa turned to Akatsuki and Keine.

"You two should go back to Elm and take the week off. You've been working nonstop for the past couple days."

"Nice! I'm gonna be honest, man, I'm pooped." Akatsuki clapped his hands in excitement, but…

"Tsukasa, if I may." Keine raised her hand slightly. "I'll be quite fine, even without rest. I have no doubts about my endurance. However, while my body will hold out, my supplies won't. I've used up just about everything I brought with me. Ideally, I'd like a facility to produce antibiotics. Can we spare the labor and funds?"

"Access to medical treatment's going to be indispensable going forward, so I'm more than prepared to get you whatever resources you need, but…are you sure you'll be okay without a break?"

"I'm certain of it. Compared to the battlefields I'm used to, being in this world is downright relaxing." At the genius doctor's smile, Tsukasa was content to take her at her word.

"Very well. In that case, send me a list of everything you need."

"You have my thanks."

"Now, Aoi, you've been working just as hard these last few days, so I'd like to let you take a breather over in Elm, too, but… I apologize for asking, but could you stay by Akatsuki's side the whole time you're there?"

"As his bodyguard, you mean?"

"Exactly. Akatsuki's the object of worship for the Seven Luminaries' faithful, so we absolutely can't let anything happen to him."

"Very well. In that case, he shall never leave my sight. I shall eat alongside him, sleep alongside him, and bathe alongside him."

"Hey, you can at least let me take my baths alone!"

"No, she can't. Aoi, make sure you stick with him even when he bathes."

"Whaaaaaaaaaaaaaaaaaat?!!!?!"

The little magician went scarlet and started voicing his vehement objections, but Tsukasa seemed content to ignore them and move on.

"Next… Ringo."

"!" Hearing her name, the scientist twitched and looked up from her phone. Her cheeks were bright red, and her expression was oddly soft. She'd been admiring the pictures Masato had sent her of Tsukasa in a maid outfit.

The young prime minister didn't quite understand what she found so persistently amusing about them, but he gave the girl her instructions nonetheless.

"I want you to start building a power plant here in Dormundt."

Ever since the Prodigies had come to this world, the seven had been getting the power for their phones and other devices from the pocket nuclear fission reactor. However, its output was gradually decreasing. Before long, that was going to pose a major problem.

Ringo's inventions and the High School Prodigies' access to long-range communications were two of their greatest assets. However, if they weren't careful, they were likely to lose both. Recognizing how pressing their need for a reliable power source was, Tsukasa had decided to build a power plant off the coast near Dormundt.

"Having access to electricity is going to be crucial for our war efforts, even more so than getting the gold from the lord's treasury back into the marketplace. I'm not expecting you to power the whole city, so it's okay if the plant is relatively small. I'm more than happy to allocate whatever manpower and funds you need. Can you do it?"

Ringo gave the matter a little thought, then tottered over to Tsu-kasa and quietly whispered in his ear. "Um, if you're okay…with a coal-powered thermal power generator…I can have it ready soon. I could also…make it hydrogen-powered…but then we'd need equipment to harvest and refine the hydrogen gas…so coal-powered…is probably easier."

"In that case, please compile a list of what you'll need and send it to me, like Keine. I'll handle getting everything ready. Merchant, your job's to assemble the raw materials."

"You got it, boss. If you can find it in the domain, my employees know where, so this'll be a cinch."

"Glad to hear it."

As soon as the prime minister finished giving his directions and the conversation came to a natural close, a voice called out.

"Teacher!!"

The blond Lyrule and the young cat-eared Roo were rushing over to the Prodigies with meat skewers in hand.

"Hey, if it ain't Roo and Lyrule. Looks like you two got your paws on something nice," remarked Masato.

"Roo grilled them herself! Have some!"

"Ooh, thanks. Don't mind if I do."

"I want one, too!" added Akatsuki. "They put mayonnaise on everything here, even the fruit. I'm sick of it!"

"Thanks to God Akatsuki's generous blessings, the whole town has fallen in love with mayo."

"And whose fault do you think that is?!"

Still squabbling, the merchant and magician took the juicy-looking kebabs from Roo and sank their teeth into them. The moment they did, their mouths were filled with a fatty, salty succulence. Fruit sauce topping the meat helped to really accentuate the flavor.

"Damn, this is taaasty. That lord really was hoarding the good stuff."

"You said it. The salt's kick works perfectly with the sauce. That's what really takes it to the next level."

"And they're only twenty rook apiece! Cheap, huh?"

""You're charging us?!""

Tsukasa grinned wryly. For better or for worse, Roo had grown quite bold. Lyrule offered the white-haired boy a kebab of his own.

"Would you like one, Tsukasa? It's free, of course." She giggled playfully.

However…

"…I'll pass." Tsukasa raised the palm of his hand to turn down the proffered food.

"Forgive me, but I have someone I need to go see. Please don't stop enjoying things on my account, though."

"O-oh."

"Who is it you're meeting?"

Tsukasa stood up and answered Keine's question. "Dormundt's captain of the guard."

…I'm pathetic, aren't I?

Tsukasa split off from the rest of the Prodigies, sighing as he made his way through the festive streets. Armed with the description he'd gotten from Heiseraat beforehand, he used eyewitness sightings from other soldiers to guide him toward his target.

Dormundt's captain of the guard, Silver Knight Zest du Bernard. There was a reason Tsukasa had taken an interest in the man. Before the Seven Luminaries came to the city, Zest had issued a firm order to all his men.

"Even if riots break out, don't you dare kill a single citizen."

Had it been a decree born of compassion? Not in the slightest. It

©Sacranecc

was merely that Zest understood. As representatives of the government, if they laid a hand on the people at a time like that, it would spark a full-fledged uprising. If the captain hadn't given that order, Dormundt would undoubtably have fallen into abject chaos. Even with his back against the wall, he'd been coolheaded enough to avoid the worst-case scenario.

After a bit of digging, Tsukasa discovered that Zest was also valorous in combat and well respected by the knights and soldiers who served under him. In short, he seemed capable and reliable—the kind of person the white-haired young man wanted to meet face-to-face as soon as possible.

That was why Tsukasa strode through the throngs of people. The young prime minister was searching for the captain. He waded through the many guardsmen who were relaxing after having been freed from the long shifts they'd endured the past few days and the citizens rejoicing at the prospect of tax overhauls increasing their income. Eventually, Tsukasa found himself in the central plaza.

Off to the side, he spotted a group of what looked to be Bronze Knights enjoying a drink. With them was a *byuma* who perfectly fit the mayor's description of the one Tsukasa sought.

"Might you be Silver Knight Zest du Bernard?" The man had a large build, and his face was adorned with a beard and an eye patch. Hearing his name, the man's droopy dog ears twitched as he slowly turned toward Tsukasa.

"Hmm? Well, if it isn't one of the angels! Apologies for not sending my regards sooner." He clearly had a good amount of drink in him already. After staggering to his feet, the knight offered Tsukasa a handshake, a loose grin on his face.

"That is what they call me. Ah, but the *du* is just a thing they stick there for imperial knights, so I guess it's had its run."

"Bernard, then. I'm Tsukasa Mikogami, but you can call me Tsukasa."

Zest gave the young man an unsteady bow, and Tsukasa returned with a handshake as he introduced himself.

"Then so I shall. What business do you have with me, Mr. Tsukasa?"

"I heard you were the one who made sure none of the city guard killed any rioters. I was curious what you'd be like. And you're exactly the kind of man I imagined."

Zest's palms were so rough and firm, it was like shaking hands with a boulder. His tirelessly tempered body told Tsukasa just how diligent a man he was. The fact that he was feigning drunkenness yet still keeping an eagle eye on Tsukasa's every move revealed the wary nature of the knight.

What's more, the looks Tsukasa had seen on the other soldiers' faces when talking about Zest spoke to the trust the *byuma* instilled. Each aspect helped paint a picture of the man.

"You give off a very different impression than the Silver Knight I met over at the lord's castle."

"No shit!"

"Yeah, 'cause Captain Bernard isn't a jackass!"

"It's rude even comparing him to that snake!"

The nearby Bronze Knights all roared in agreement. Zest quieted them down with an exasperated wave of his hand, then thanked Tsukasa.

"Well, it's an honor to hear you say that."

"...Now I know I can rest easy entrusting you with this."

"With what?" Zest tilted his head to the side.

"Ah, that's right," Tsukasa started. The reason he'd come in search of the captain of the guard was—

* * *

"Bernard, I want you to serve as the commander of our army, the Order of the Seven Luminaries."

They were no longer the ragtag band they'd been when they'd attacked the lord's castle. Prisoner knights and soldiers were in their custody now. Plus, those warriors who'd initially fled but surrendered upon realizing that no one else was likely to pay them were under the Prodigies' control, too. Most recently, they'd acquired Dormundt's city guards.

Having a strong leader was going to be crucial if the Prodigies wanted to unite them into a single, cohesive army and entrust them with carrying out the will of the Seven Luminaries. As this new nation grew, so, too, would its army, making the matter all the more essential. Tsukasa felt that Zest was the man for such a job.

"The Dormundt city guard you led comprises more than half our newly assembled force anyway, so I can't imagine anyone more qualified than you. What do you say?"

"…I—" Upon receiving such an appointment from Tsukasa, Zest began mumbling evasively. Before he could say much, though, the two found themselves interrupted.

"Papa!" A young, female voice caught their ears. Zest was the first to react to it. The knight raised his head, and when he saw the young *byuma* girl dashing over to him, his face lit up.

"Airi! What's going on? I thought you were playing with your friends."

"I came looking for you with Coco!"

"My apologies, sir. You were clearly in the middle of a conversation, so I tried to stop her, but…"

A middle-aged woman with skin the same color as Roo's came running after the girl. She bowed apologetically. Zest waved her down, unconcerned, then gave Airi a big hug.

"Why were you looking for me, sweetie?"

"I found something yummy!" The girl, Airi, presented Zest with the small apple pie she was holding. Such confections were one of the many things being offered during the festival.

"You brought this just for me?"

"Yup! Say 'aah'!"

"Aah… Wow, you're right. That is tasty. Thanks, sweetie!"

"Hee-hee-hee. You smell like beer, Papa." Airi nuzzled Zest's beard happily.

Having suddenly found himself thrust into a domestic sitcom, Tsukasa tried to clarify the situation. "I take it this lovely young lady is your daughter?"

"Yup! Airi is Papa's Airi!"

"…She's my little treasure and the only thing I have left of my wife after she passed in the epidemic." Zest kissed his daughter on the cheek, then gave her back to Coco.

Not finished with his business, the knight urged the two of them to go on without him.

Coco took Airi by the hand, and the girl obediently followed, having finished what she'd set out to do. With a farewell wave to her father, Airi and her caretaker vanished into the crowd.

Zest watched them go, then turned back to Tsukasa and gave his response to the earlier proposition. "*Imperial knight* has a nice ring to it, but even if we Bronze and Silver Knights are technically nobles, we're really no different from the rest of the common soldiers.

"We serve a lord in exchange for coin, same as them. Amount's different, maybe, but not much else. And without those wages, we'll starve just as quick as anyone. So if a new master comes around, I'd do anything from leading their army to cleaning their toilets. Got a daughter I need to protect, after all.

"But the thing is…this whole 'knight' gig's just a means to that end. What I'm sayin' is, putting her in harm's way just ain't an option for me. Even if the emperor himself ordered me to, I could never abandon my family.

"So as you can see, my loyalty doesn't amount to much. You don't want a guy that pathetic commanding your army, do you?"

In short, Zest's apologetic declaration meant the man was willing to lead if Tsukasa ordered him to. However, the *byuma*'s loyalty wasn't such that he'd be willing to sacrifice his family in the line of duty.

Basically, it was an indirect refusal. As Zest saw it, he'd be better suited to remain as Dormundt's captain of the guard so as to keep protecting his daughter's home. The knight lacked the loyalty required for a higher post—especially the commander of an entire nation's forces.

"You fight for the sake of your family. There's nothing pathetic about being a devoted father." Tsukasa answered the rebuttal with a rejection of its very premise. Surprise crossed Zest's face as the white-haired young man continued.

"There exist people who brainwash others into thinking that strangers like *kings* and abstract concepts like *nations* are more important than anything, even their own families. They even use violence and force to coerce people into dying for them. As far as I'm concerned, though, that's nothing more than state-sponsored homicide. And it's utterly unforgivable.

"The government's role shouldn't be to brainwash its soldiers into easy-to-manipulate pawns or to enact cruel laws to prevent people from challenging it. A politician's job should be to work hard making a country that other people feel is worth putting their lives on the line for."

Tsukasa had never been interested in seizing Zest's loyalty through coercion and tyranny. He was searching for a collaborator who wanted to live alongside the rest of the people in the new world the Seven Luminaries were building.

"Zest Bernard, all I ask is that you keep fighting for your daughter's sake, as you already are. The onus is on me to convince you that leaving this nation for your daughter is a deed worth risking your life for. And I swear to you that's a task I intend to put my heart and soul into."

The drunken haziness had vanished completely from Zest's eyes. Tsukasa wasn't forcing the Silver Knight to pledge his allegiance or trying to extort loyalty from the *byuma* with a promise of punitive violence. It was the first time anyone had ever put so much *trust* in the man.

When Zest saw how earnestly Tsukasa was treating him, he finally realized he'd been laboring under a misconception—that he'd simply be working for a new master. That's how he'd regarded the Seven Luminaries, but that was wrong.

The nation this upstart new group was hoping to build wasn't going to have hierarchies like that anymore. Every person who lived in that new society would be their own master. Truly, that was the kind of country this strange group was working toward. A world where everyone had the freedom to choose their own path.

Ahh, that'd be…that'd be a wonderful place to live indeed. The thought crossed Zest's mind reflexively.

As someone with the power to fight, it was his duty as a parent to throw himself into the fray to help build that world for the sake of his daughter's future. Kneeling to bow before Tsukasa, the Silver Knight swore an oath.

"I accept this great responsibility with all that I am."

"Glad to hear it. I'm counting on you."

After securing Zest's assistance, Tsukasa elected not to return to the other Prodigies but to instead look around the city for himself.

He'd heard that Count Heiseraat had governed relatively well, but the citizens still seemed overjoyed at the succession of the Seven Luminaries. Good mayor or not, having a feudal lord who collected outrageous taxes had put a considerable strain on the livelihoods of the citizens. If nothing else, the fact that the High School Prodigies had ousted the lord and promised to revise the tax code alone made them heroes among the people.

However, everything the commoners gained came with corresponding losses to the nobility.

"..."

Quite suddenly, Tsukasa felt piercing, hostile looks bearing down on him from a side street. When he turned, the white-haired boy caught the angry glares of several men. Their classy outfits made their identities immediately evident—nobles who lived in Dormundt's High-End Residential District.

The instant Tsukasa's eyes met theirs, the men turned and made their way back toward their homes via the alley. Even though it had only been a moment, it was enough for Tsukasa to see just how strong their seething dissent was.

Such was to be expected, though. Vested interests always pushed back against reform. Over time, their opposition would only grow fiercer.

Tsukasa had hoped to fill out the government with nobles, the educated members of the former society, but...only those suited to the task. The young prime minister had no intention whatsoever of offering them money and status merely to pacify them. Furthermore, he fully intended to punish those who had levied exorbitant taxes and committed inhuman acts against the peasantry during Marquis Findolph's reign.

That was likely to earn even more backlash from the wealthier folk. A fundamental problem was that the nobility considered commoners to be no better than worms. They didn't think of them as fellow human beings. It was a mindset etched into them since early childhood.

In other words, the kinds of morals and ethics that served as deterrents back in Japan didn't apply here. The rich could truly do anything.

When such people sought to vent their hatred and frustration…

…there was no telling what acts of cruelty they were capable of.

There are still ripples spreading across Findolph's surface. I hope nothing serious happens, but…

In any case, Tsukasa knew that he needed to keep an eye on the nobles' movements.

At the same time, in a different place.

Squeezed between the Findolph domain and its neighboring territory sat a sea and the Le Luk Mountain Range. Shinobu Sarutobi, accompanied by Elch, had sneaked through Le Luk and infiltrated the neighbor in question—the Buchwald domain.

"Golly gee, they're saying there was a revolt over in Findolph and the lord got strung up. Is that true?!"

"Yeah. I heard it from some soldiers who fled from there, so you know they're telling the truth."

"It makes sense, honestly. Up there in the sticks, they've got the mountains protecting them, so no war's ever gotten that far north. Their soldiers ain't got shit for training or equipment." At the moment, the *kunoichi*-journalist was in a tavern in Elmer, an inn town at the base of the Le Luk chain.

Disguised as a waitress and working under the pseudonym "Mimi," she was pumping a group of Buchwald soldiers for information.

"Oh heavens. But what if those big, scary rebels attack us next...?" The girl clutched her shoulders and feigned terror. The men grinned wide at her seemingly meek demeanor, and the act helped loosen their tongues.

"Don't you worry your pretty little head, Mimi. That's what we're here for."

"Yeah, and it's not just us. Once winter passes, Buchwald's main forces are gonna join up with a big army from our neighbors, Archride. Then, when spring rolls around, we're gonna march on the rebels and pound them into dust."

"The Fastidious Duke wants to go crush them right away, though."

"Yeah, but that shit ain't happening. Trying to cross Le Luk at this time of year is suicide, and the Dragon Knights can't even fly when it's this cold out."

"The Fastidious Duke's a city slicker. He has no idea how brutal the mountains are in winter."

"But anyway, Mimi, there you have it. We ain't gonna let nothin' happen to you!"

"Oh, well, shucks. I feel safer already!"

"Hey, no fair!"

"I'm telling your wife about this when we get back!"

One of the soldiers leaned over and wrapped his arm around Shinobu, an act that earned a few angry shouts from his colleagues. However, the one member of the group nursing his beer said something in a low voice.

"...Yeah, but even if we didn't invade, you'd still probably end up fine."

"How do you mean, mister?"

"I heard this all from a soldier who came seeking refuge three days ago, but apparently, these rebels...they're with some church called the Seven Luminaries. It's trying to push equality and close the

gap between commoners and nobles. The rich see them as enemies, but the poor see them as allies. Word is they're doing a decent job of getting rid of the shitty, biased tax system, and they've even raised wages for guardsmen... Honestly, I'm a little jealous."

"Hey, man, pipe down." The faces of the other men at the table grew stern. If their superior heard them, the man was likely to get decapitated. However, the soldier seemed unconcerned.

"It's fine. When Old Man Kendra drinks, his hearing's the first thing that goes." The man who spoke of treason gestured with his thumb at the table behind them.

Their superior, an aged Bronze Knight, was sitting there, but his bright red face broadcast that he was wasted. The old man was too busy trying to grope his waitress's butt to pay their conversation any heed.

"And besides, just 'cause I'm jealous doesn't mean I'm gonna betray the empire over some silly pipe dream... Once the Fastidious Duke makes his move, it'll be over for those guys."

"Yeah, you can say that again."

"This 'Fastidious Duke' you all keep mentioning... That's the lord of the Gustav domain, right?"

"Yup. You know, Mimi, you really know your stuff. Good on you!"

"Tee-hee... So what kind of person is Lord Gustav?"

The answers the disguised Shinobu got made the man sound like some sort of legendary historical figure.

"Oh, he's incredible. Oslo el Gustav is a martial genius and a master mage, and in the war against the Yamato Empire, he stood on the front lines himself and slaughtered wave after wave of enemies. In recognition for his valor, he was the first knight in the empire's history ever to be made a duke and given authority over an entire region. Now he's the Warden of the North. The man's fiercely loyal to the emperor and demands that others show the same degree of fealty. Because he's such a perfectionist, folks call him the Fastidious Duke, and he never shows a shred of mercy to any who go against the emperor… That's the sort of guy who holds the office of the Warden of the North. In the four northern domains, rebels aren't safe anywhere."

At around nine that night, Shinobu finished cleaning up the tavern, ate dinner, and headed back to her inn. When she opened the door, she sensed someone inside. It was someone she knew—specifically, Elch, who'd tagged along to aid her intel-gathering mission.

"Oh, El-El, you're back. Heya."

The only light in the room came from the fireplace. Now that Elch realized Shinobu was back, he tried to sit up from where he was sprawled out on the bed.

"Mm, yeah… I just got…———!!" Halfway through his sentence, though, he let out a silent scream. The young *byuma* man had spent the last few days riding around on horseback, using a map of dubious quality to navigate from village to village in search of information. As a consequence, his crotch was chafed raw.

"Don't force yourself. You can just stay on your back."

"I might just take you up on that…" Elch flopped back down.

When she looked closer, she saw that his tail was twitching. He must have been in a lot of pain. What better time to find out what fruits his labor had borne?

"So you hear any juicy stories?"

"Nah, just the same rumors about an army mobilizing once winter ends."

"Anything about the Seven Heroes or the real Seven Luminaries?"

"Nothing. Most people didn't even know that's what we've started calling ourselves."

"Hmm. Well, I guess that's what you get in an era with no mass media."

However, between what Elch had heard and the information Shinobu herself had gathered in the tavern over the past few days, they could be more or less certain that the army was waiting until the snow melted before beginning their march.

"Anyway, good work. I'm gonna go let Tsukes know what's up. Once they know for sure they don't hafta worry about the army till spring, it should give them some breathing room."

Shinobu reached down to pull out her smartphone. Before they left, she'd gotten its battery and signal both strengthened. As the girl was about to grab it, however, Elch suddenly remembered something.

"Oh, that's right. I've got something else, but it doesn't really have anything to do with us."

"Oh? Well, don't keep a girl waiting!"

"Apparently, the Buchwald's had an uptick in commoners trying to flee from the Gustav domain. The ones who don't make it are killed and left for the crows in front of the checkpoints... It's pretty nasty. Gustav's supposed to be the most beautiful domain in the empire, but all those corpses must make it look like a den of demons."

"Huh. That's all news to me."

Elch was right: None of that information was important to their situation. And yet—

Oslo el Gustav, the Fastidious Duke, huh...

—given what the soldiers had said, it would seem he was the one putting the army together.

Gustav was unflinchingly loyal to the empire and refused to abide any who opposed it. The man's brutality and devotion were all too apparent from the way he'd treated the peasants who'd tried to escape his rule.

Equality. There was a good chance a man like Gustav was

fundamentally incompatible with the notion... At some point, they were going to have to face off against him.

And one side's not making it out alive...

Furthermore, not only was he in charge of the region, he was also a powerful Prime Mage. That was going to be a problem, too. Magic didn't exist on Earth, so it was difficult to estimate how effective it would be in war. If they went in against him blind, they were liable to suffer unexpected losses. That was something Shinobu wanted to avoid. To do so, the journalist member of the Prodigies was going to need to get to work.

"Well, nothing ventured, nothing gained, they say. That settles it!"

"Settles what?" Elch cocked his head quizzically. Shinobu gave him a wink.

"I'm gonna go meet this Fastidious Duke for myself, duh!"

CHAPTER 2

❦ Lyrule's Melancholy ❦

Angels don't sleep. Or at least, that was the rumor that had made the rounds in Dormundt a few days after the Seven Luminaries took over the city. It started because of the way in which Tsukasa carried out his municipal work from the office he'd fashioned out of the library in the mayor's mansion. As the Seven Luminaries' brain, he enacted a number of different reforms.

A revised tax system that had previously served merely to line the nobles' pockets, legislation that abolished the noble-commoner-slave class system, and the creation of educational institutions and the appointment of intellectuals to them, disseminating knowledge to the masses. Each was significant, but the list of changes hardly stopped there.

"Getting rid of institutional inequality is the bare minimum requirement for a functional democracy."

Such was Tsukasa's stance.

Over the course of that process, he had to converse with a number of intellectuals and former nobles. Strangely, though, no matter what time his visitors came to the office, they invariably found him working.

He was there from before the sun rose to late at night when even the plants lay dormant. At some point, someone came up with a theory as to why that was.

"Angels don't need to sleep," they'd hypothesized. Of course, that wasn't the case in the slightest.

Tsukasa might have been from another world, but he was just as mortal as anyone else. When Mayor Heiseraat asked him about the hearsay, the white-haired boy's reply was nonchalant: "I don't rest before I get to work. I rest after I've finished."

In order to rewrite the entire legal system from the ground up, he was making the ex-noble government officials toil day in and day out to get the job done. It wouldn't be fair unless he worked even harder.

Eventually, a week had passed since the Seven Luminaries took the city.

Once again, Tsukasa was consumed by work. However, his office was empty. Instead, he was off checking on the progress Ringo had made on her power plant.

They'd wanted to ensure the fire wouldn't spread to Dormundt if there was an accident, so they'd built the generator off the coast, about two miles from the city.

Tsukasa was heading there via his private carriage.

"We're here, Mr. Tsukasa."

"Uhh…ah, thank you."

Hearing the driver call his name, he awoke from his brief catnap and stretched a little. The driver looked at him in astonishment.

"There's no way a nap that short in a carriage this rocky did you a lick of good. Can't you just take a day off or something?"

"Not while I'm pushing everyone else to their limit for the sake of these reforms. Me working hard enough to make them think angels don't sleep is good for morale. 'Looking like I'm doing my job' is part of my work in and of itself. So remember, the fact that I doze off on these carriage rides is our little secret." Tsukasa raised his index finger in front of his lips to emphasize the point. The playful gesture earned him a strained smile from his driver.

"…Why don't we take the scenic route on the way back? You can call it a city inspection or something."

"You know, when I hired you as my personal driver, somehow I knew I was making the right call. I have a meeting waiting for me after this, so though I have to decline the offer, I appreciate the sentiment nonetheless."

Tsukasa opened the carriage door and stepped out. When he did, the prime minister was immediately met with a greeting.

"Ofur here, Tsukasa!"

The voice he heard wasn't human but electronic.

It belonged to the plant's foreman, Ringo's all-purpose support robot—Bear Rabbit, or Bearabbit for short.

Skillfully maneuvering the spiderlike manipulator arms that extended out from his backpack body, the artificial intelligence made his way over to Tsukasa. Masato, who was in charge of supplying materials, was with him.

"Well, well, well. Looks like we've got a bigwig riding in on his carriage to conduct a site inspection."

"Some dunce decided to get the whole city addicted to mayonnaise without considering the consequences, so I've been up to my ears dealing with the salmonella poisoning caused by bootleg mayo. It's just been one thing after another." After giving his retort, Tsukasa turned his attention to the bustling site of the power plant.

Great groups of people, largely composed of freed slaves who'd elected not to go back to work for their old owners as well as residents of nearby villages who were bored out of their minds due to there being no work in winter, were working to construct a rectangular building equipped with giant smokestacks.

Eventually, it was going to be Dormundt's new power plant. The brick outer walls were almost complete. There was basically nothing left to do other than finish installing the smokestacks and triangular anti-snow roof.

"Wow. I'm impressed you all were able to build this much in a single week without any heavy machinery."

"It's hard to make money during the winter, so people were champin' at the bit to work. We basically just threw manpower at the problem."

"The site was all clawttered with the snow yesterday, but they all pulled through anyway."

"I'm glad to hear the people are so motivated. A country is only as strong as its workforce, after all. By the way, is the generator installed yet?"

"Yep. Ringo used the last of our battery pawer to get it up and running. Once the roof and chimneys are in, we'll be ready fur business."

"We've got tons of coal to use as fuel, too." Masato indicated the mound of black rocks covered by a tarp to keep off the snow. All in all, the pile was probably a good ten feet tall.

"All of that is coal?"

"Everyone knew you could burn it for fuel, but they also knew how toxic the fumes were. When they go mining, they usually just end up throwing it out, so I was able to pick it up for almost nothing."

"That's what I like to hear. So how long until the plant starts running in earnest?"

"At this pace, we'll be in a pawsition to do a trial run tomorrow. The pawer's set up to get stored in the high-capacity battery we salvaged from the pocket nuclear fission reactor, so that should solve our energy problems."

"I'm glad to hear it. Electricity is one of the few big advantages we have in this world. Once that gets up and running, we'll be able to proceed with the next operation."

"Which is?"

Tsukasa thought for a moment, then made his choice. He'd been keeping his plans under wraps so their workaholic teammate, Ringo, wouldn't push herself too hard. However, Masato was the one in charge of collecting raw materials. It was better not to leave him in the dark.

"I'd like to modernize part of our army in preparation for the battles this coming spring."

"Modernize? Meaning, you want them bearing firearms?"

Tsukasa nodded.

"I've already asked Bernard to put together a special unit—a hundred soldiers, handpicked by him. Bear Rabbit, I need you and Ringo to build a factory next to the power plant equipped with lathes, milling cutters, drill presses, and everything else you need for machine work. I want to create a space where *the people of this world* can manufacture guns and ammo *by themselves.*"

A big question mark popped up on Bearabbit's display.

"Would it be a problem if Ringo and I had a paw in making them?"

"Not as such, but the people of this world were the ones who started this war. They need to be the ones to continue it. That's why I want them as involved in the process as possible.

"Given the state of this world's technology, simple bolt-action rifles and break-action shotguns should be sufficient for our purposes. They're similar to the guns this world already has, so if you explain how to build them and use the machine tools, you should be able to set up a production line without having to get directly involved after the fact."

"…Yeah, that's probably for the best. We might have subjugated Dormundt, but a bunch of the former nobles are still pissed as hell.

It's like we've got little powder kegs sprinkled all around us. If we give this world machine guns all of a sudden, any sort of revolt they threw would get ugly real fast."

"That's certainly one reason, but...I also have other projects I need Ringo and Bear Rabbit to put their considerable scientific prowess and productivity to work on. Things only they can do."

"Like what?"

"For example, building the equipment and bags to store blood for transfusion like Keine asked for this morning. Also, I need you to start working on an air-defense system."

"You mean, like, ground-to-air missiles?"

Tsukasa nodded.

"From what I learned from the books I dug through and the chat I had with the mage we captured back at the castle, this world's magic comes in two forms:

"The first is small-scale tactical magic. It's akin to tactical arms. It's quick, single-phrase spells that can do things like 'summon gusts of wind that can cleave through metal,' 'shoot bullets of ice,' and 'create bursts of flame large enough to blow up a house.'

"The other is large-scale war magic. This kind is more like strategic arms. It requires rituals that take years to perform, but one spell can raze an entire town.

"There are only a few people in the empire who can use war magic, but...the mayor says the man commanding the army against us—Warden of the North Oslo el Gustav—is one such individual. A few years ago, when he was fighting the now-defunct Yamato Empire, he was able to use Heavenly Fire to engulf the enemy's base in a sea of flames from an entire mountain away...or so the tale goes."

"Heavenly Fire, huh? I see... So that's what you're trying to guard against?"

"Ideally, although we won't know if missiles will work until the moment arrives. However, according to Shinobu, this world has both magic and people who ride dragons into battle. Simply put, they have access to aerial warfare. That means we can't leave our skies undefended… Can you do it, Bear Rabbit?"

Bearabbit gave Tsukasa an energetic reply.

"You can depanda on me! Now that we have materials aplenty and a reliable source of electricity, the sky's the limit! Once we finish the power plant, Ringo and I will start with the machine tools before moving on to the rest of the list!"

"Good. I'm counting on you."

Just as their conversation reached a natural stopping point, someone new cut in.

"Tsukasa!"

A cheerful female voice called out to the young prime minister from behind. When he turned around, Tsukasa saw Lyrule's golden hair bobbing up and down as she dashed over to him. The white-haired boy's eyes went wide in surprise. He hadn't expected her to be there.

Once they'd realized that the empire was unlikely to retaliate until after the snow melted, Winona and most of the other Elm residents returned to the village to rest. Tsukasa had been under the assumption that Lyrule had gone, too.

"You didn't go back with Winona and the others?"

Lyrule shook her head as she answered. "No… I was what started this whole war, so I wanted to try to be of some use to everyone. Today, I was helping prepare food for the workers."

Now Tsukasa understood why the blond girl had stayed. The rest of the villagers were the ones who'd decided to go to war, so there was no need for Lyrule to feel guilty, but her brain simply didn't work that way.

Realizing that, Tsukasa responded, "Thank you. I appreciate you lending a hand."

"Oh, it's no problem. It's something I wanted to do," the girl replied a bit bashfully. "But, um…" After a brief moment of silence, she steeled her resolve. "…I was actually about to go have lunch. Would you like to join me?"

"With the workers, I presume?"

"Mm-hmm. We prepared plenty of food, and also…I still haven't properly thanked you…for what you did back there."

What I did back there. Tsukasa sensed Lyrule was referring to him saving her back at the lord's castle.

After the siege, Tsukasa and the others had to immediately get to work taking over the domain, so he and Lyrule hadn't had a decent chance to talk since. The young woman was probably still hung up about what he'd done for her.

However—

"You're too kind, really…but I'm afraid I have to decline."

—he turned down her offer. Just like he had on the evening of the festival…

"I haven't put in the labor, so it wouldn't be right for me to take food meant for the plant's workers. Also, I have a meeting with the nobles who used to manage Findolph's towns and villages that I need to get to."

"Oh…"

"I do appreciate the sentiment, though." With that, Tsukasa sauntered off at a brisk pace. The white-haired young man found he was disgusted with himself all the while.

As she watched Tsukasa disappear into the distance, Lyrule felt her heart pound. He was just busy. That was all, right? As the guy calling the shots, Tsukasa was spending sleepless nights working. All that was true.

It was all true, but Lyrule sensed from Tsukasa's reply there was something else going on. She'd noticed it during the festival, too.

Rejection.

He was avoiding her and being distant. Could it be...?

"Masato, does...does Tsukasa hate me?" Lyrule turned toward the businessman, her voice full of unease.

"Nah." Masato laughed. "There's no way. He just has a lot on his plate right now."

"I know that, but...it's just...I feel like it's more than that. It seems like Tsukasa actively doesn't want to spend time around me..." The girl's eyes swam with worry. Her insightfulness made Masato break out into a cold sweat.

Damn, girl, you're sharp.

He could tell she'd be a dangerous person to cheat on. As a matter of fact, her hunch was on the mark. Masato knew Tsukasa well enough to be able to tell what was going on.

Right now, the boy was actively trying to distance himself from Lyrule, and Masato could tell why, too. However, the master merchant also knew it wasn't his place to say. Masato had tried to play dumb, but...

"Is he...is he mad that this whole war is my fault? You all aren't even from this world, but we went and got you wrapped up in our problems anyway."

"You weren't the one who made the call, were you? I'm sure that doesn't have anything to do with this."

"So what is it? Does he think my weird ears look creepy or something...?! Or is it—?"

"Hey, calm down. It's fine. Nobody hates you, Lyrule."

"But...but...uwaaaaaanh!" All of a sudden, the blond young woman grabbed her long ears and began sobbing in large droplets.

"Huh?! Hey, c'mon, that's not something to cry about!"

"I'm just—I'm just so *worried*..." Lyrule's reaction made Masato falter.

He'd never imagined that Tsukasa's rejection was taking that heavy a toll on her heart.

"..." Masato let out a small sigh. He couldn't just keep quiet, not after seeing the face she was making. After all, Lyrule wasn't the one who'd done anything wrong.

Look, dude, you're the asshole here. This shit's your problem, not mine.

After internally cursing Tsukasa a little, Masato went ahead and told Lyrule the truth.

"...Yeah, okay, you're right. He *is* avoiding you."

"R-really?!"

"Don't worry, though. You didn't do anything wrong. This one's a hundred percent on him. Back when everyone in the village was raring to go save you, he was the only person who wanted to abandon you to your fate."

"Huh...?"

"That's why it hurts so bad for him to talk to you. Doubly so because you're trying to thank him for it." The businessman laid bare Tsukasa's reason for avoiding the girl.

Rather than surprised, though, Lyrule merely looked perplexed. Tsukasa had been the first to rush in and save her, so she'd never considered the possibility that he'd originally wanted to abandon her.

"Is...that so...?"

"But hey, don't be too hard on him for it. It's not like he didn't want to save you or anything, and he definitely doesn't hate you. Look, if he hated you, would he really have chosen to take a job as dangerous as charging deep into the enemy's stronghold himself? That dumbass's bad habit just kicked in, that's all."

"Bad habit? What do you mean?"

"No matter what's going on, he always puts the well-being of the majority first.

"When the inhabitants of a feudal society rise up against the ruling class, it never ends cleanly in immediate victory or reconciliation. No matter how smart you go about it, a revolution's always gonna leave mountains of corpses and rivers of blood in its wake.

"Tsukasa knew that could all be prevented by throwing you under the bus. He knew that if he choked back a couple tears, countless innocent lives would be saved. That dude's the kind of guy who'd say that out loud to a bunch of hotheads who just wanna rush in and snatch you back.

"Just so you know, it's not because he doesn't care about you or anything. He'd have said the same thing even if it was about his own flesh and blood. If it's for sake of the majority…even if that's a bunch of people he doesn't know, that guy would go so far as to sacrifice his own parents."

Ah…

Lyrule felt her blood go cold. She'd heard the same thing from Tsukasa's own mouth. He'd killed his own father and shattered his family for the sake of justice for the masses.

"I've known the guy since we were kids, but I still don't get it. What's so bad about putting your own interests first? Is it really so wrong to abandon others for your own benefit?

"Why should we have to sacrifice ourselves and the people we care about just for some randos? I could never be like that. I don't want to be.

"But Tsukasa doesn't waver. It didn't matter how badly he wanted to save you; he pushed those feelings down and gave up on you to protect a bunch of people he'd never even met... I mean, we're not talking something positive like kindness or benevolence here.

"If I'm being honest...the guy's completely *crazy*."

No human being could think like that. No living creature could think like that. Maybe something had gone wrong in Tsukasa's head somewhere. Perhaps he was just born that way. It was hard to say. One thing was clear, though: He was broken on a fundamental level.

However, Masato said something else, too. The businessman told Lyrule that Tsukasa Mikogami's inhuman mindset was exactly what made him the political genius he was.

After he'd finished, Masato flashed her a smile.

"...Anyway, what I'm getting at is that Tsukasa's a certified weirdo. But he doesn't hate you, and you didn't do anything wrong. That dumbass is just self-destructive. Leave him alone for a bit. He'll come around."

In a way, Masato's self-deprecating smile had been a kind of plea. He was being considerate, in his own way. Considerate of his awkward, ruinously sincere friend. Masato was asking Lyrule for a favor. He was asking her not to thank Tsukasa.

The blond girl had sensed as much from his expression and tone—

"No."

—but refused to comply.

"Huh?"

"Thank you, Masato. Now I know full well what kind of person Tsukasa is."

Masato hadn't expected her to shoot him down so firmly. He

scrutinized her face in surprise. The young businessman noticed something as he did—Lyrule's clouded expression had vanished. Now her eyes and mouth were brimming with determination, and her eyebrows were almost bristling.

"…Wait, Lyrule, are you *mad*?"

"Yes, I am. Very mad, in fact. To borrow a phrase from your world that Shinobu taught me—" Lyrule paused for a moment to take a deep breath.

"I'M AS MAD AS HELL, AND I'M NOT GOING TO TAKE THIS ANYMORE!!!!"

Her shout was so loud and frustrated that all the construction workers looked up from their work for a moment to see what was going on.

"Damn…that's pretty mad."

"Yes, it is. Once I'm finished here, I'm going to go give Tsukasa a piece of my mind." Lyrule squared her shoulders up in anger as she headed back to her job. Masato let out a regretful sigh as he watched her go.

"She's a sweet girl. Too sweet for that blockhead, that's for sure. Hell, if she were a bit older, I'd be all about that." Tragically, though, she was too young to be Masato's type. He was only into women at least a decade older than him.

"Too bad," he murmured again. Beside him, Bearabbit plastered a teasing smile on his display.

"You're beary sweet, too, you know, clearing up your friend's misunderstanding like that. Oh, what a beautiful thing male friendship is…"

"…"

"Hmm? What's wrong? Why are you taking out that Sharpie— EEEEEEK!! That's barbearic! Quit vandalizing my touch screeeeeeeeen!!!!"

That night, even though it was very nearly the next day, Tsukasa was toiling away in his office.

"I'm so sorry, but there simply wasn't any way for us to verify the age on some of the buildings... We took the estimates our craftsmen made based on their exteriors and listed them in parentheses, but there's no guarantee those are fully accurate..."

"..."

A young *hyuma*, a former baron, stood across the desk from Tsukasa, giving him a report that was filled more with excuses than actual information. As the prime minister sat half listening to the man, he used the candlelight to glance over the accompanying documents the *hyuma* had delivered. After a while, Tsukasa looked up.

"...I see. You did well. This is plenty."

The *hyuma* breathed a sigh of relief. Fatigue was etched across his face. It had probably been several days since he'd gotten a decent night's sleep. Tsukasa decided to offer him some words of appreciation.

"Thank you for all your hard work. Take tomorrow off so you can rest up."

The ex-baron bowed, then left the library. The moment he was gone, Tsukasa heard gleeful cheers from the other side of the door. They belonged to the carpenters the man had been working alongside.

"Thank goodness, it's finally over..."

"Man, my legs are killing me..."

"We were all gonna go for a drink after this, Baron Royce. You wanna come?"

"…I'm not a baron anymore, but I'll gladly take you up on your offer. I've never really had a chance to chat with you fellows before."

Tsukasa heard their footsteps grow distant. Based on their conversation, he could tell the perceptions among the people of Dormundt were gradually starting to shift.

Not long ago, the nobles and commoners had lived completely disparate lives. The fact that the whole group was going off to drink in the same pub was a sign that things were changing for the better.

It was the government's job to get rid of unjust laws and eliminate disparities caused by arbitrary things like bloodlines. However, it was ultimately the citizens themselves who needed to come together and create a common sense of values and unity.

Government intervention on that front would only be counterproductive. They needed to reconcile their differences through repeated interaction. Giving the same tasks to people of different social standings and opening up opportunities for them to see eye to eye was the extent of what Tsukasa could do.

Of course, the nobles whom Marquis Findolph had put in charge of running small towns saw themselves as rulers. They were unlikely to change their ways as quickly as the likes of Royce and the other nobles who had merely worked as bureaucrats under Mayor Heiseraat. That was a problem for another day, however.

"…In any case, that was today's final report." The moment he said the words aloud, Tsukasa felt his vision waver.

Unfortunately…it seems I've hit my limit.

It had been bound to happen sooner or later. Altogether, the white-haired boy had only gotten ten hours of sleep over the past week. Furthermore, all of it had taken place in roughly half-hour increments on shaky carriage rides. Such rest was hardly enough to relieve the fatigue his body was accumulating.

Even though the people of this world were the ones who'd willed it, he and the others had definitely played a role in starting the conflict that would go down in history as the People's Revolution. In other words, it was Tsukasa's responsibility to make sure that the war, as well as the vast amount of bloodshed it would bring, ended up holding meaning for future generations.

He'd used that thought to drive himself up until that point, but everyone had a limit. Tsukasa was used to pushing himself to impossible levels, so his true maximum was something with which he was well acquainted. That's why the young prime minister could tell if he went any further, his body would break.

That was no good. Not only would it impede progress on the reforms, it would make the people start doubting the Seven Luminaries' angels.

I don't have any more meetings tonight, and after tomorrow's morning briefing, I have those negotiations with the nobles who felt their punishments were too severe. I'm going to need my stamina for that... I wanted to finish making some progress on the library's documents on magic, but I guess I'd better sleep instead.

Tsukasa decided to allow himself a brief respite. With three hours of sleep, he'd be able to make it another three days. However, right as Tsukasa was about to stand up from his chair, he heard a noise.

Someone was knocking on his door.

"Who is it?"

"It's me, Lyrule. There's something I really need to talk to you about... Are you free right now?"

Tsukasa expression darkened. He knew full well why Lyrule was calling on him at that late hour. It was Tsukasa who'd saved her back at Findolph's castle, and she wanted to thank him for it. The young man could tell she'd been trying to do so for the past few days. That was precisely why he had been avoiding her.

Back then, he was the one who'd proposed leaving her to her fate. Such a person was hardly worthy of being thanked. Nothing about that fact had changed.

"…I apologize, but I have another busy day tomorrow and need to get some sleep while I can. Some other time, maybe—"

"I understand completely. If you're going to sleep, that means you're done with work for the day."

"Hmm?"

"I'm coming in!" Lyrule threw open the double doors with a *bang* and barged into the library.

"Wh—?" Tsukasa gaped at her, not expecting her to employ such an aggressive tactic. The blond girl, on the other hand, kept striding toward him, cutting around his desk.

"L-Lyrule, is whatever this is really that urgent?"

"Yes. I've been trying to thank you for coming to my rescue in the castle this whole time, and you've been running away from me. I need you to let me thank you properly!"

"I-I'm afraid I don't quite follow…"

"You can ask me for anything. As long as it's within my power, I'll do it." The girl drew even closer to Tsukasa, then struck a defiant pose right in front of him. Lyrule was so close that if he stood up, their foreheads would bonk.

Tsukasa could see fierce determination glowing in her blue eyes. She'd made up her mind. The expert politician could tell that the time for false pretenses was over.

And so—

"…I was ashamed and didn't want to say it out loud, but… I'm not the one who saved you. When Winona and the others tried, I told them they were being rash… To put it bluntly, I wanted them to abandon you. I even called your lack of relatives *convenient*. That was where my mind went."

—he told her the truth about his attempt to turn a blind eye to her crisis.

Tsukasa knew that Lyrule held some amount of affection for him. At the end of the day, what was done was done. If he could have avoided telling her, that would have been for the best. The boy had no desire to be hated, after all. Yet, even so, he didn't have it in him to accept gratitude he hadn't earned.

"I'm in no position to receive your thanks."

Even when faced with his confession, however—

"Yes, I know that already."

—Lyrule didn't so much as flinch.

"What?"

"But that doesn't bother me in the slightest. Back then, what you tried to do was what I myself wanted. If sacrificing me meant the village would be safe, I was fine with that.

"But...when you came and saved me, it made me so, so happy. I was scared. When Lord Findolph touched me, it made me so sick I couldn't take it.

"So whether or not you think you deserve my thanks is irrelevant. I'm the one who gets to choose whether to thank you or not! So...I'm going to thank you as much as I want! And I'm not leaving until you let me show you my gratitude!"

Lyrule grabbed Tsukasa, still sitting, by the shoulders and loomed over him. Her slender fingers seemed determined not to let go.

"...I can't say I'm fond of how pushy you're being."

"I'm not happy about it, either, but I have to. Otherwise, you won't even let me thank you."

"I was ready to offer you up to Findolph."

"But you saved me anyway, and you held me tight. I can still feel your warmth from when you did. I still remember how kind you were. So no matter what happens, I won't hate you! You might think it's perfectly natural for others to despise you, but I'm never going to feel that way, no matter how much you think I should! If you don't want me being so forceful, you'll have to push me away with all your might!"

"..."

Tsukasa found himself at a loss. He'd never expected her to be so persistent...and he *certainly* hadn't expected her not to hate him after learning about the heartless decision he'd made. Quite honestly, Tsukasa was flummoxed.

Was it really all right for him to take advantage of her kindness? Could letting her forgive what he'd done really be okay? He'd been the one to advocate leaving her for dead. Tsukasa still wasn't sure. One thing was certain, however.

The moment he heard Lyrule's words, sensed her emotions, and felt her *joy*...had been the moment he'd lost their stubborn little argument.

"...You win. I surrender." Tsukasa let the tension drain out of his shoulders.

"Besides, if I tried to push you away from this position, I suspect it would constitute sexual harassment."

"Huh... Hwa-wa-wa!"

It took Lyrule a moment to realize what he meant, but when she did, her face flushed red. The young woman was pinning him from above—her breasts were hanging right in front of his face. If Tsukasa had wanted to push her off, he would've had no choice but to grab something untoward.

Yet, even as the girl went crimson to the tips of her ears, she refused to back down. Tsukasa looked up at her in exasperation.

"Having regrets yet? I'm not nearly as accommodating as Masato. There's nothing for you to gain by doing this."

"That's...for me to decide."

"…I suppose so. Once again, you're absolutely right." Tsukasa gave her response a strained smile.

Lyrule's stance was far more logical than his. She had him beat on all fronts. As a matter of fact, Tsukasa was the one in the wrong for trying to get her to share his guilt. Realizing that, the prime minister saw he had no choice but to humbly accept her thanks.

"You'll really do anything, then? Even something somewhat laborious?"

"Of course. As long as I'm able!"

"In that case, would you mind sitting down on that sofa for me?"

"The sofa?"

Tsukasa's eyes looked over toward a couch large enough to seat four people. Lyrule tilted her head to the side, unsure what Tsukasa was getting at, but she went over and sat down as instructed.

"Like this?"

"No, all the way on the end— Yes, right there." As he spoke, Tsukasa headed to the large piece of furniture himself and sat down beside her.

Then—

"Oh!"

—he rested his head on her lap.

"…Ah, this is comfy. Far better than an actual pillow."

"Um, Tsukasa, what's this about…?" The young man's sudden action had made Lyrule visibly surprised and embarrassed.

"You said you'd do anything, so I was hoping you'd help give me an hour of sleep. How does that sound? With a pillow this comfortable, I could get three hours' worth of sleep done in just sixty minutes."

"…Ah." Lyrule had been bewildered but now saw what he was getting at. Smiling sweetly, the young woman accepted the request.

"Of course. I would even give you the whole night, if you want."

"That would take quite a toll on your legs."

"Oh, I'm fine. It would be one thing if we were on the floor, but this is a nice sofa. And compared to how much gratitude I feel toward you, one night is nothing."

"If you say so," Tsukasa replied, accepting Lyrule's insistence. "But if your legs start cramping, don't hesitate to wake me."

"I will. Good night, Tsukasa."

"Mm… Thank you…" With that, the young man closed his heterochromatic eyes. In no time at all, his breathing grew more regular as he fell into a deep, restful slumber. Surely he must have been dead tired.

"Ah…"

When Lyrule looked at his sleeping face, she noticed something. There were dark circles around his eyes that Tsukasa had been hiding with makeup. He really had been pushing himself to his breaking point. And it had all been for the sake of Elm Village and the rest of the people of this world.

As Lyrule came to understand this, gratitude began welling up within her so intensely that she nearly started to cry. At the same time, it made her heart feel tight.

…I want to become someone he can depend on…

It troubled Lyrule that all she could do for Tsukasa was give him a lap pillow. For now, however, the blond girl was going to do just that until he awoke on his own, even if that didn't happen until morning.

Someone peeked through the door and looked at Lyrule and Tsukasa.

It was someone who'd come to hand over a list of materials they needed to manufacture guns as well as to suggest that it might be more technically efficient to come up with an entirely mechanical system for mass-producing the ammo and grenades: Ringo Oohoshi.

"_____"

Lyrule was affectionately stroking Tsukasa's hair as he lay on the girl's lap. When Ringo saw that, a silent scream quivered in her throat. Ever since an incident back in middle school, she'd had a crush on the young prime minister.

That was precisely why Lyrule's expression told Ringo everything she needed to know. She could tell that Lyrule held the same feelings for Tsukasa that she did.

The scene playing out beyond the door came as an utter shock to the genius inventor. In fact, it was so bad that she wanted to rush in and put a stop to it. However, Ringo also knew just how exhausted Tsukasa was. She couldn't bring herself to give in to jealousy and interrupt his gentle slumber.

Instead, Ringo choked back the cry rising in her throat and turned around. Then she left, heading back the way she'd come.

"Mrrrrrgh—" All the while, her cheeks were so puffed up that she looked like a hamster with its mouth stuffed with food.

That moment marked the first crack in the High School Prodigies' otherwise-harmonious relationships with the people around them. For the rift to form between Lyrule and Ringo, two women so demure that nobody would expect either of them to get into a fight with anyone, was truly a surprise.

This fracture ended up sparking some minor turmoil. However, that wasn't bound to happen for a while yet.

©Sacraneco

CHAPTER 3

⚜ Roo's Multiplication Matter ⚜

Tsukasa and the others were out bringing reform to Dormundt.

Winona, having returned to Elm Village, was treating the wounds Ulgar had sustained in his battle against the monster known as the Lord of the Woods.

"Wow, this is really something. The wound's already almost completely closed." It was hard to imagine it coming from an attack that had sliced his guts to ribbons. As Winona unrolled the bandages and disinfected the wound with alcohol, she marveled at Keine Kanzaki's handiwork. "And the stitch is so clean, it probably won't even leave a scar. That Keine kid is something else."

Ulgar, who'd awoken from his coma the week before, was currently wincing a little from the sting of the disinfectant and made no effort to mince words.

"You know, you could learn a thing or two from her. You sew up people like you're sewing up dishrags."

"It's fine, it's fine! Having a few dozen scars makes a guy look more handsome anyway."

"For heaven's sake, hun… You saying stuff like that puts the beauty you inherited from your late mother to waste. If you don't learn some delicacy, how will we ever find you a new husband? There's this little thing called tenderness, y'know. Ever heard of it?"

"Don't go setting your sights too high, now. I'm *your* daughter, after all. There, your new bandages are all…set!"

"OW!" Ulgar let out a pained yelp as Winona slapped the man's back hard enough to leave a handprint.

"And besides, this is no time to be thinking about marriage. We just picked a fight with the empire, y'know."

"…A lot happened while I was out, huh."

"Yeah, you missed your chance to show off."

"Ha-ha, that I did." Ulgar laughed heartily. Not once had he criticized the decision they'd made. After all, he was pretty sure he would have done the same if he'd been in their shoes.

"I gotta get better quick so I can go join the fight."

"Don't go trying to act cool, Pops. Leave the bravado to Elch and enjoy your retirement."

"…Elch, huh. He's off helping young Shinobu sneak into Buchwald right now, yeah?" To Ulgar, that had been the most surprising development since he'd regained consciousness.

Elch was clever and good in a fight, but because of that, he had a bit of a calculating side to him. Ulgar could hardly believe that same grandson of his had agreed to go on an espionage mission.

"He's gotten brave of late."

"He's your grandson and my and Adel's son, you know. The boy knows how to pull through when it counts. And besides," Winona added with an ill-natured grin, "I think he has a thing for Shinobu."

"Oh-ho! Should I expect them to come back with a great-grandchild in tow?"

"Ha-ha-ha, I doubt it. My gut tells me she's been around the block a few times. That virgin boy of mine's probably just gonna end up wrapped around her little finger." Winona laughed her father down, then stood up and gave her tail a light shake to straighten out her fur.

"I'll bring lunch over, so you just stay there and rest up." The woman headed toward the door leading out of the shed they were staying in, in lieu of the mayor's burned-down house.

Before she could get there, though, she heard the sound of creaking wood coming from the other door leading farther inside. She and Ulgar both turned to look, but neither was particularly surprised.

Although the closet had previously been used to hold farming implements, they both knew it had been cleared out so someone could live there. Winona called over to its inhabitant cheerfully.

"Roo, did you want to come have lunch with—?!"

Her tail sprang up in alarm. Roo had come crawling out from behind the door on her hands and knees, so gaunt she looked like a desiccated cat corpse.

"So…hun…gry…bleh."

""Roo?!?!""

"Whew. Roo's alive again. She's been brought back from the dead."

The little girl breathed a sigh of relief. Now that they'd fed and rehydrated her, her body had made like a dried shiitake mushroom submerged in water and returned to its original volume.

Winona got right to business. "How many days were you cooped up in there? There's such a thing as being too diligent, y'know."

"I'd just assumed you were using the room's other door to go straight outside. I had no idea you were in there the whole time. What were you doing, skipping all those meals?"

"Teacher..." Roo's triangular cat ears slumped as she answered their questions. "Teacher gave Roo some tests she needs to take. He told Roo she can't come back to the city until she gets a perfect score on the multiplication test... He said that times tables make it easy to remember, but Roo's having trouble with that, too..."

"What's a 'times table'?"

"Teacher said it's a trick that helps you remember how to multiply."

"You know about this, Pops?"

"Can't say I do. Never really had much of a head for letters or numbers."

"Ha-ha, me neither. I just left all that to Adel and Elch. But hey, Roo, chin up. You don't need letters or numbers to lead a good life! Just look at us!"

"Right! We're doing fine! Gah-ha-ha!" Winona's and Ulgar's dog ears perked up as they laughed merrily. When Roo looked at them, her young heart was seized by a pang of apprehension.

Roo doesn't know why...but she's pretty sure if she listens to them, she's not gonna turn out too good.

"Anyway, I dunno what to tell you about all that stuff, but first things first." Winona pulled out a linen towel from a nearby drawer and tossed it to Roo. "You haven't had a bath since you came back to Elm, right? We've got a hot spring now, so why not take a dip? Nothing like getting clean to clear your head."

Roo hesitated. After all, if she had time to take a bath, she'd rather spend it studying. However, even she could tell that staying cooped up in that room wasn't doing her ability to concentrate any favors. Also, she reeked, and her hair was all oily and gross. The former slave made up her mind.

"...Okay. Roo will do that..." As Winona had suggested, Roo decided to start by taking a bath.

"One by four is four, one by five is five, one by six is six…"

In order to get in a better headspace, Roo had gone over to the hot spring Tsukasa, Aoi, and Bearabbit had built on the riverbank, but when someone was in a rut, relaxing was easier said than done. Roo floated in the water, her head still swirling with numbers.

However—

"Two by four is eight, two by five is ten, two by six…pick up sticks…?"

—no matter how many times she repeated the times tables like Masato had taught her, none of it stuck.

The numbers are all just floating around. Can't get them to stick in Roo's head… All she was doing was single-mindedly listing the calculations off one after another. Doing that made it all feel too abstract, and she would quickly lose focus. The girl's issue wasn't confined to just multiplication, either. Back when she was working on addition and subtraction, she'd felt the same.

"Math doesn't make any seeeense!" She kicked her legs aimlessly, splashing water all around her as she grumbled. Then, her ears picked something up.

"Don't look, okay? Make sure you don't look until I say you can! You promise?!"

"I read you loud and clear, m'lord, so hurry up and strip."

Roo could hear two familiar voices coming from the hot spring's newly added changing room. It was Prince Akatsuki and Aoi Ichijou, two of the people who'd returned to the village with her.

"…Look, can we please not go into the bath together? It's super embarrassing."

"This is a battle you've long since lost. At the moment, you are akin

to our daimyo, *that you are. Having a bodyguard by your side at all times is but common sense."*

"Man, why is this happening to me…? You know, for a break, this hasn't been restful at all."

"Why not simply ignore me and relax as though I were not here?"

"Trust me, I would if I could! …All right, I'm ready on my end."

"I have been ready for some time, that I have."

"Cool, let's get in the—WH-WH-WH-WHY ARE YOU NAKED?!"

"Hmm? Does one not always remove their clothes when bathing?"

"Not when it's a mixed-gender bath! You're supposed to cover yourself up with a towel or something!"

"As a child of Edo, I despise such effeminate notions, that I do!"

"Quit power posing like that! And besides, you're a girl, so you should try to be at least a little effeminate!"

"Oh, enough with your whining already! Just get in the bath—!"

"HWAAAAH?!"

All of a sudden, there was a kicking sound, and Akatsuki hurtled through the changing room's curtain.

"Gweh?!"

Then, he landed directly in front of Roo, who'd been listening intently to their conversation, and a huge wave erupted before the girl.

"You have my deepest apologies. I had no idea there was another bather here. I've not brought you injury, have I?"

"N-no. Roo's fine. Just a little startled."

The young girl shook her head from side to side to get the water off.

"Akatsuki, m'lord, none of this would have happened had you not put up such a fuss."

"Y'know, that's weird. I could have sworn I was one of the victims, yet here I am getting blamed. Something doesn't add up." Akatsuki averted his gaze from Aoi's immodest figure, bubbles rising from his mouth as he complained with half of his head underwater. As far as the magician was concerned, it was clear Aoi was the one who'd taken things too far. Still, they'd gotten an innocent bystander wrapped up in their spat, so he knew he should apologize nonetheless.

When he turned to the victim in question, though, he noticed something unusual.

Roo's expression, which was normally as bright as the sun in the tropics, was decidedly glum.

"Hmm? What's got you down, Roo?"

"Now that you mention it… Are you quite certain you're uninjured, m'lady?"

"Roo's fine… She just has a lot on her mind…"

"Do you want to talk about it?"

"…Well, actually…"

The other two were worried about her, so Roo went ahead and told them about how she was having trouble with multiplication. Akatsuki and Aoi nodded sympathetically. They'd both suffered through the same thing back in elementary school.

"Times tables, you say. Ah, how nostalgic."

"Yeah, right? We had to learn those back around second grade, too, Roo."

"How did it go again? Three by one is three, three by two is six, three by three is…do-re-mi?"

"Wait, are you serious?!"

"Ha-ha. The truth is, that was around the time I began devoting myself solely to the blade, so I know little of numbers beyond addition and subtraction."

"How did you make it to high school like that?!"

"I am a student athlete, that I am!"

©Sacranec

"Student athlete programs everywhere should sue you for slander!" While Akatsuki offered pointed comebacks to Aoi's assertions, Roo bobbed her way over to him.

"Akatsuki, do you know the times tables?"

"I mean, I might be bad at schoolwork, but even I know the times tables."

Roo grabbed his shoulders, her eyes glistening. "P-please, teach Roo! Teach Roo how to learn them!"

"Uh, I'm not really sure how… Well, for starters, multiplication is just taking the same number and adding it up a certain number of times. Like, three times one is the same as taking one three. Three times two is two threes, so it's three plus three, so it's six. From there, you can just add one more of the original number each time."

"Yeah… Teacher told Roo that, too…" Roo already knew that conceptually, but when she used it to multiply something like three times nine, she'd end up with so many threes, it made her head spin.

"So Roo ran out of time on the test, and she didn't pass…"

"Yeah, that's why we use the times table to shorten that long process. Hmm, I guess repeated memorization might be your only option. If you don't know your times tables, multiplying two-digit numbers is a nightmare."

"Oh no…" Roo's ears slumped. She submerged her face up to her nose. The thought of having to keep memorizing that weird chant was depressing.

Seeing how much anguish the little girl was in, Aoi offered her a kind smile. "You know, when I see you working so hard to become a merchant, it reminds me of my own days in training, that it does. I recall being utterly fed up with having to repeat the same forms time and time again."

"Oh yeah. Learning magic is all about repetition, too, so I know how you feel," Akatsuki remarked. "And because I know how the tricks work, it's not even all that fun."

"You two were the same as Roo...?" The young *byuma* knew that these two, as well as the rest of the High School Prodigies, were all experts in their fields. However, she hadn't considered that they'd gotten to that point by going through the same tedious process she was currently experiencing for herself. Such a revelation made Roo curious about something.

"How did you two stick with it?"

Aoi's answer didn't take much thinking. "I had an objective, that I did."

"What's an 'objective'...?"

"Something you want to do or perhaps something you want to gain. When I was a child, I watched a period drama called *The Unfettered Shogun*, and it made me want to take up the sword to protect the powerless. That meant I needed to train, so I did."

"And you, Akatsuki?"

"Yeah, basically. By the time I was in elementary, I already knew I was going to become a magician. It was the only thing I could really see myself doing."

"...Roo has something she wants to do, too." After hearing their stories, the girl remembered she was the same. She and her parents had been loaded onto separate slave ships, but she was going to buy them back and live with them again. That was why she was becoming a merchant. It was why Masato had bought her, for an amount that made Roo's head spin, no less.

"Nyaaaah!"

The little girl gave her cheeks a loud clap.

When she thought of those lines of artificial numbers, it had made her light-headed and caused her to question why she was even bothering. But Roo couldn't let herself complain about something as insignificant as that. She had a dream, after all. The only way to achieve it was by overcoming her current hardship.

"Roo's gonna try her best, too! She's gonna learn her times tables, even when they're boring, and she's gonna beat multiplication!"

"Very good. That's the spirit, that it is." Aoi rubbed Roo's newly invigorated head.

As Akatsuki watched them from the side, a lightbulb went off in his brain. "Hey, Roo, what's your favorite thing?"

"Money!"

"Uh…okay. Well, that works. If you're having trouble just thinking of numbers, why don't you try thinking of them as gold coins instead? Five times five can be five stacks with five coins in each, that kinda thing."

"—!"

Hearing Akatsuki's suggestion made Roo feel like something had just gone off in her mind. The five stacks of five coins had appeared like a vision in her mind, and she knew instantly there were twenty-five of them in all.

"Roo gets it! She can beat multiplication without needing to use times tables now! Give Roo a problem!" she begged Akatsuki.

"Okay, what's two times nine?"

"Eighteen coins!"

"Hey, you got it right. Good job."

"Another! A harder one, this time!"

"All right, well, here's a tricky one: seven times seven."

"Forty-nine coins!"

"Wow, seriously? Okay, here's a nasty one: three hundred and sixty-five times twenty-four." "Eight thousand seven hundred and sixty coins!" "Geez, that was fast!"

It was the only problem using the hundreds column that Akatsuki knew the answer to off the top of his head, and Roo had answered it without breaking a sweat. Even Akatsuki, the one who'd proposed counting gold coins in the first place, was shocked. He hadn't expected it to work nearly that well.

"Wow! I know not whether you got it right, but that was impressive nonetheless!"

"N-no, she definitely got it right... I guess when you do what you love, success really *does* follow."

"Roo gets it! She gets it now! Roo's finally conquered multiplication!" The girl leaped around the bathtub excitedly.

Akatsuki knew that her innocent exterior belied a worrying degree of avarice. The magician pondered for a moment if he'd made the right choice, but the girl herself seemed so happy that he decided not to think too hard about it. Besides, she was already Masato's disciple. That alone meant she was beyond saving.

In any case, though, Roo successfully mastered not just her times tables but even triple-digit multiplication, allowing her to pass her test that day with flying colors. Masato gave her the go-ahead to move on to the next step.

...However...

The next day, when Aoi and Akatsuki went to the dining hall to eat their breakfast, they found Roo looking up at the snowy clouds. The light had completely faded from her eyes.

"..."

"...Hmm? Akatsuki, m'lord, I thought Roo passed her multiplication test. Why do her eyes look like those of a fish washed up on the shore?"

"Well, y'see...her next test's on division."

"...Ah. The merchant's path is an arduous one, that it is."

"Too true."

"Roo's money… All her coins are splitting up and shrinking… Division is scary…too scary…" For genius businessman Masato Sanada's finest student, Roo, the former slave girl, the long road to riches was only just beginning.

Ill-Boding Flames

"To hell with that albino freak!"

The snowfall was heavy that night.

Over in Dormundt's High-End Residential District, an angry voice could be heard, along with the sound of something getting kicked. A well-dressed young man with wolf ears was throwing a drunken tantrum.

"Angels? Gimme a break! He sure looks like a normal guy to me! Dammit, I wanna pummel his stupid, girly face until it looks like a potato!"

"Kyle's temper seems worse than usual today..."

"I don't blame him. Viscount Niersbach, his father, was prosecuted and imprisoned by the commoners. They even stripped him of his right to govern Ravale, an authority originally granted to him by Marquis Findolph."

The raging drunk, Kyle, was accompanied by two others of similar dress. One was bespectacled and looked more intellectual, while the other was chubby and seemed rather meek. Each was a former noble who lived in the High-End Residential District.

"It's a crying shame," the bespectacled young man said in reference to the fate of Kyle's father. "But soon, our days of biding time will be over, and our counterattack can begin."

At those words, Kyle spun around from where he was kicking at a stone wall. "You mean, you got the goods?"

"Huh? What are you two talking about?"

"My family and the Archride family are distant relatives. They sympathize with our situation, so they sent us something to help… Namely, these."

With an evil grin, the bespectacled young man pulled a round pot out from under his coat.

"What's that, some sort of pottery? If it is, it looks a little crude."

"Of course it does; it's full of gunpowder. It's a bomb they call Roaring Thunder."

"A—a bomb?!"

"Not so loud, moron! But still, I'm surprised you were able to sneak them in. Shipping those things over during the night is one thing, but getting bombs into the city proper must have been tough."

"Oh, not at all. The commoner swine are only wary of us nobles."

"You mean, you used peasants as mules?"

"Of course. And we're running the whole operation through their filthy hovel of a residential district, so our efforts should go undetected for some time."

"I-I'm surprised you got those peasants to side with you."

"Heh… Equality might seem nice on the surface but leads to a world that's harsh on the incompetent, and there's no shortage of incompetents among the commoners." The man was right. Not all the commoners were on board with the message the Seven Luminaries were spreading.

Some people just wanted to leech off the nobles. Others doubted their own abilities and feared the prospect of a society built on competition. More still simply didn't trust the Seven Luminaries themselves.

There were folk of many minds on the subject. The bespectacled noble had gathered such people and used them to sneak the bombs into the city.

"When spring comes, and the subjugating army with it, we'll use catapults to blanket the town in these things. The Seven Luminaries will find themselves hit from both sides."

"Heh, I'm looking forward to it. I can't wait to watch that albino punk crap himself."

"B-but…if we do that, the commoners might actually kill us…"

"What are you talking about?! We're nobles! We have justice on our side!"

"Quite right. The emperor is sure to be most pleased with our hard work. You're a member of the imperial nobility, too. It's time to start acting like it."

"O-okay… Yeah, you're right."

The trio continued making their way down the darkened street.

"Huh? What's that?"

Right in front of them, they saw a strange structure cast in the moonlight. It was like a little unfinished hut built right off the side of the road. It had a roof and supports but only two walls. The glasses-wearing noble looked down at it.

"Ah, it's one of the shrines the Seven Luminaries have been building around town of late."

"What's a shrine?"

"A word of Yamato origin. They worship some idol called a *jizou* by way of these little huts."

"Huh. So what, they've got a little statue of that blond kid in there?"

Curious, Kyle walked over to the half-built hut and popped in through one of the unfinished walls.

However, it was too dark to make out anything clearly.

"Tch. I can't see for shit. Hey, Marco, gimme some light in here."

"S-sure."

The plump noble lit up his lantern.

Now that it was illuminated, Kyle could make out a large, cylindrical pillar inside the hut.

"Huh? What's this supposed to be?"

"...Yeah, why's it a cylinder?"

"It certainly doesn't look like a statue..."

"Heh-heh-heh. I figured it out, guys. Those lowly savages don't have the technology to carve statues, so they just stuck a big rock here instead to try and trick us."

"That seems eminently plausible. Primitives are fond of their stone circles, after all."

The two of them let out scornful laughs.

"Guess we don't have a choice, huh? As representatives of the empire's greatness, it's our job to teach them a thing or two about class."

Kyle turned the wine bottle he was holding over and poured its contents onto the pedestal on which the cylinder was enshrined.

"You like that? Tasty, huh? Nothing like the stale wort you paupers drink. This here is sweet, mellow, full-bodied booze. The finest stuff around. Drink up, O mighty God of the poor savages! Ha-ha!"

Suddenly, the three heard something. The sound of metal on metal and footsteps treading on the fallen snow.

"Kyle, someone's coming!"

"I recall hearing that they assigned guards to their little shrines, so I suspect it's that."

"Tch. It'd be a pain if they found us here. Let's bounce."

Kyle and the others quickly left the unfinished hut and vanished down an alley. Not a moment later, the bespectacled noble was proven right, as the guard returned.

"…Whew. Man, when it gets this cold out, the ol' bladder starts working overtime…"

The young, shivering soldier had no idea. He hadn't the slightest hunch just how much his little mistake would contribute to the coming tragedy.

CHAPTER 4

⚜ Infiltrating the Gustav Domain ⚜

It had been around a month now since the Seven Luminaries took over Dormundt. Shinobu Sarutobi and Elch, for their part, had just made it into the Gustav domain. The shallow snow on the footpaths crunched pleasantly under their feet. Up ahead, they could make out a small village. Shinobu suggested they find lodging there, and Elch readily agreed. It was only just past noon, but in order to sneak past the checkpoint, they'd spent the previous two days sleeping in the snow-filled forest. It was doing a number on their stamina.

From where they stood, the village looked like it couldn't possibly have more than a hundred residents. It might not have had proper inns, but for some coin, the two could likely guarantee a room of some kind over their heads, at least. With that thought carrying them forward, Shinobu and Elch made their way onward. Eventually—

"No way…"

"What *is* this place…?"

Arriving at the village, they couldn't believe their eyes.

"Th-this is…nuts. And this is just a little farming village?"

"Merely by crossing the border, it's like we stepped into a whole other world…"

They knew about all the commoners who'd tried to flee from the region, so the two of them had envisioned the Gustav domain as some sort of awful hellscape. Sure, they'd heard it was the most beautiful place in the whole empire, but it was assumed that only held true of the big cities. They'd expected the smaller villages to be ruins filled with worn-down farmhouses.

However, that assumption stood in stark contrast with the scene before them. There wasn't a speck of dirt anywhere to be seen, and all the farmhouses were covered in pastel coats so bright, it seemed as though they'd just been painted.

Furthermore, the streets were all neatly paved with milky-white stone brick, and streetlamps were installed at regular intervals. To top it all off, the town square was adorned with an intricately carved fountain.

The two travelers were dumbstruck.

"This is unreal, El-El. I mean, look! All the houses have glass windows!"

"Yeah, and they even have a fountain… Who knows how much that must have cost…?"

It was like being in some sort of high-society garden. Yet, in spite of that, it was just a common farming village. The splendor of the buildings wasn't the only impressive thing about the town, either. As they wandered about gawking at their surroundings, the passing villagers all called out to them.

"Good day!"

"Good day! Fine weather today, no?"

"Good day! Welcome to Coconono Village!"

Each villager bore a sociable smile and offered Shinobu and Elch cheery greetings. The people were just as amiable as the scenery was pleasant. More than just smiles and welcoming attitudes, their clothes were nice, too.

These weren't the bundles of cloth the Findolph and Buchwald villagers wore to stave off the cold. No, these were colorful, well-coordinated outfits and dresses. The fabric wasn't just plain linen, either. It was adorned with lace and gold trim. Nothing too outlandish but still was nothing peasants should have been able to afford. In fact, not even nobles would own items like that unless they were dedicated fashionistas.

"They still seem like commoners, but it looks like they've got it pretty good here."

"Yeah. So it does..."

The two both let out amazed remarks about the Gustav domain's unexpected wealth. Then, they heard a voice.

"Look, we have guests! Emelada, over here!"

An elderly *hyuma* man called after a young *byuma* woman and a girl of about ten, both with bear-like ears.

"Good day, travelers!"

"Good day!"

The woman and girl both offered Shinobu and Elch small bows. Other villagers had passed them by and gone on their way, but these three stopped to greet them. The two weary travelers stopped in turn and returned the greeting.

"Good day to you, too. I gotta say, you're all real friendly here."

"As a small rural village, we don't have much to offer visitors, so the least we can give them is hospitality." The young woman smiled as she made the jest, then gave them her name. "Oh, I should introduce myself. I'm Emelada, and this here is my daughter, Milinda."

"These two run the town's inn. The sun'll be setting soon, and the next town over's a fair bit away. Why don't you stay the night at their place? You're the only customers today, so all the rooms are open." It appeared the old man had gone and summoned the proprietor of the local lodgings for them.

"Wow, thanks for the help! Staying at an inn was our plan all along, so you saved us the trouble of having to look for one."

"Oh, is that so? Well, glad to be of help." The toothy grin the elderly *hyuma* flashed them was oddly white and shiny. When Shinobu looked, she could tell his teeth were artificial. They seemed to be carved from ivory or the like. The technology to mass-produce such things didn't exist in this era, so they must have been as valuable as jewels.

How was this tiny village able to sustain such a high standard of living? As questions swirled through Shinobu's mind, young Milinda happily called out to her.

"Hey, miss, mister. Are you two married?"

Elch's cheeks went scarlet. He immediately opened his mouth to deny it.

"There's no—mmph?!" However, Shinobu clamped her hand over his mouth.

"Tee-hee, yup! We're a traveling entertainer couple!"

"HmMMmmM?!"

"It's too fishy to have a young guy and gal traveling together if they aren't married. Just play along."

"O-oh, okay..."

After Shinobu whispered in Elch's ear, he realized the ninja-journalist was right and quickly agreed to her cover story.

Not a moment later—

"Wow, that's great! Hey, fellas! Apparently, these two are traveling entertainers!"

"Whoa, seriously?!"

"That's so cool! What kind of tricks do you do?! You gotta show us!"

—the two found themselves surrounded by excited villagers.

The old man who introduced them to Emelada and Milinda made them an offer.

"What do you say? Would you be so kind as to show us your stuff? There's no fieldwork to be done this time of year, and we don't get too many merchants, neither. Most of us are bored sick. If you put on a show for us, we can repay you with food and booze!"

"Are you sure?"

"Oh, please do. My daughter would love it, too. I'd be happy to let you stay the night for free in exchange."

Had they just offered free room and board? Shinobu gleefully accepted.

"You guys drive a hard bargain, but sure, we'll do it! Right, El-El?"

"Uh, sure…?"

"Huzzah! Everyone, make preparations for a feast!"

"You got it! Today's gonna be great!"

And thus, the two of them ended up trading a display of their talents in exchange for free food and a place to sleep for the night. The part about them being traveling performers was a lie, but they *did* both possess specialized skills.

Shinobu elected to juggle some borrowed pottery while balancing atop a ball, while Elch showed off his masterful archery by performing tricks such as shooting a snowball off of his companion's head. Both were met with hearty applause from the villagers. The young Milinda was especially enthusiastic, hopping up and down and clapping so hard that Shinobu and Elch were worried the girl was going to hurt her hands.

As thanks for their performance, the villagers threw them a lavish feast. There were meat skewers dripping with juices, stew full of hearty sustenance, and plenty of sweet beer to go around.

At the villagers' urging, Elch downed tankard after tankard of the drink. Before long, he noticed his head feeling fuzzy and his body feeling hot. It went down so easy, the young man hadn't noticed it at first, but the beer must have been fairly strong. The smiling villagers praised them for their skills and refilled their steins.

It was unclear if Shinobu realized it was alcoholic or not, but the atmosphere being lively, she was gulping the stuff down like there was no tomorrow. Elch, swept up by the mood, emptied his own mug in kind. By the time the sun started setting, the two of them were well and truly plastered.

After the lively reception dinner, Milinda and Emelada led their inebriated guests to the inn. In keeping with the rest of the village, it was built from tidy red bricks and boasted an impressive chimney. Off to the side, it had a wooden stable to accommodate visiting merchants. An unmanned wagon was resting inside, almost ornamentally.

"Wheeee... The world ish melting... Like cheeeese... Hee-hee-hee."

"C'mon, Shinobu, keep it together... Hic..."

Elch tried to tell off the journalist, who had gotten so drunk he'd had to carry her to their lodging on his back. However, the beer had made his face so red and his gait so tottering that it looked like he needed the advice just as badly as she did. Emelada gave a concerned bow as the pair approached.

"Are you two all right? I'm so sorry. We tend to get a little carried away here."

"No, no... I'm fine..." Elch groaned.

"Yeah, I'm jusht peachy! I can keep going all night! ...Urp."

"Hey! Don't go throwing up on my back, you hear!"

Struck by an ominous premonition, Elch set Shinobu down. She covered her mouth, face pale.

"Hwehhh... Why doesh it feel sho good and sho bad at the shame time?"

"'Cause you were downing the beer like it was water, that's why. Not that I'm anyone to talk, mind you."

"Urrrgh… I'm gonna go outshide to get shome air…"

"Oh! Th-that door doesn't go outside!"

Shinobu staggered straight toward the wooden door in front of her, but Emelada quickly stopped her and lent her a hand.

"The door outside is over here. Milinda, Mom's going to keep an eye on Shinobu, so could you be a dear and show Elch up to their room?"

Milinda nodded.

"Thank you, darling," Emelada replied as she led Shinobu outside.

"And shank *you*, Msh. Emelada. You're sho nishe…urp!"

"Oh my! P-please don't throw up until we're actually outside!"

"Is…she gonna be okay?"

Elch turned around, worried, but Milinda called for him and bade the young man to follow her. The girl led him up to the second floor.

"Here's your room."

"Ah, thanks… I had a bit too much to drink, too, so I'm gonna go ahead and lie down. Standing makes me feel faint." Elch sat down on one of the room's two beds as he thanked Milinda. As he did, though, he noticed something.

Hmm…?

There was a hint of trepidation in the *byuma* girl's expression. Her smile from before was gone…and her eyes were swimming as though she was agonizing over something. Then…

"Mister…"

Milinda looked at Elch as though she'd made up her mind.

"You have to hurry and get out of—" She was trying to tell him something. However, the girl wasn't able to get the end of her message out. Emelada had come up the stairs with Shinobu in tow.

"Thank you for showing our guest his room, Milinda."

"…"

The moment Emelada showed up, Milinda went silent and scampered down to the ground floor. Emelada, who was lending Shinobu her shoulder, took her place.

"Is Shinobu…er, my wife okay?"

"Oh, she's fine. Once she threw up, she seemed a lot better."

"It feels like I'm floating on a cloud…" The moment Shinobu made it into the room, she plopped herself drunkenly onto the floor. The High School Prodigy might not have needed to throw up anymore, but she still looked pretty wasted.

"Sorry for all the trouble…"

"Oh, not at all. If anything, it's our fault for encouraging you to drink so much." Emelada chuckled wryly. "But please, make yourselves at home." She gave the pair a slight bow, then exited the room and closed the door.

After Emelada had left, Elch summed up his thoughts on the village. "Y'know, I was worried about how things'd go after we made it over the border, but this village actually seems really pleasant. Their buildings are nice, their clothes are fancy, and everyone's really friendly… I'd expected all the commoners to be wearing shabby stuff like we do, but I guess things are just different here, huh."

From what he'd heard during the feast, the villagers were largely wheat farmers. As they'd happily explained, they didn't have much income, but because of how well Emperor Lindworm von Freyjagard and Lord Oslo el Gustav kept the peace, they were able to live in comfort despite that.

Honestly, Elch had trouble believing it all. He could never have imagined commoners in the empire being so blessed with luxury.

"It looks like they've got it pretty good here, so I dunno how excited they'll be about the Seven Luminaries' teachings. Got any backup plans?" Elch had directed the question at Shinobu.

However, instead of an answer—

"Zzz... Zzz..."

—the only response he got was snores.

When he looked, he saw her lying facedown on the floor.

It appeared she'd never actually made it onto the bed.

"Wait, are you seriously asleep...? Man, what am I gonna do with you?" Elch sighed in exasperation, then drunkenly tottered over to Shinobu to lift her onto the bed.

"C'mon, now. If we don't at least get a blanket on you, you're gonna catch a cold."

The next moment, though, something unbelievable happened. Shinobu's arms shot up and wrapped themselves around the back of the young man's head. When she yanked him toward herself, their lips met.

"Mwah. ♡"

"MmmmMMmph?!?!?!"

They pressed deep against each other. The girl's mouth was hot from the alcohol. Elch froze up, unsure how to process what was happening. What was going on? Should he have done something? However, he quickly returned to his senses and pushed Shinobu off. He voiced his objections with a bright-red face.

"Wh-wh-wh-wh-what's the big idea?! Y-you! Drunk or not, y-you can't just—?!"

"Well? All sobered up now?"

"Huh...?" Elch found himself at a loss for words. This wasn't the reaction he'd been expecting at all. He'd thought that Shinobu was so plastered that the girl didn't know what she was doing. Judging by her expression, however, she didn't seem intoxicated in the slightest.

"You...aren't drunk?"

"Of course not. It'd take more than that to get a ninja sloshed. Besides, I made sure to take a liver supplement beforehand." Shinobu's tone was the same as ever. She was well and truly sober. But if that was the case, then why...?

"Why the act, then?"

"If I didn't fake it, they'd have kept bringing out drinks until I really *was* wasted. Didn't you notice? The villagers were all trying to get us to live it up, but they barely touched their own drinks at all."

"Wait, why?"

"That's what I wanna know. Why were they so insistent on getting us drunk? Plus, their houses and clothes were clearly expensive, but all the people... *Why do they look like they're starving?*"

"They do?"

"Their heavy winter clothes did a good job of hiding it, and they were using makeup to make their faces look presentable. Their skin was all dry and ragged, though. Even an amateur could make out the jaundice in their eyes." Such symptoms were typical of malnutrition.

The first time Shinobu had set eyes on the villagers, she'd caught on immediately. Something about the village was fishy.

"...It wasn't until we got to the inn that I realized *why* everything was so weird. C'mere."

"Wh-where are we going?"

"Through that door I tried to go through before... Don't worry. When I was pressing my ear against the ground earlier, I made sure our two hosts were gone." Shinobu left the room and moved briskly toward the door in question. It was down the stairs and past the service counter.

When opened, the two found a stairwell leading down. Using Shinobu's smartphone as a light, the pair began their descent. Before long, they found themselves in front of yet another door. Shinobu paused before it and turned to Elch.

"El-El...no matter what we find here, you can't scream. Got it?"

"O-okay." Elch nodded, and Shinobu pulled the handle toward herself.

Elch felt a cold sensation run down his spine. The cause was easy enough to deduce: the smell. The moment Shinobu opened the door... the rank smell of blood assailed his nostrils. The young man's eyes went wide as morbid curiosity made him wonder as to the source of the horrible odor. The *kunoichi*-journalist shone her light into the room.

Inside—

"_____???!!!"

"This here...is the village's secret."

—they saw them.

Cast in the light against the dark background were brutalized human corpses dangling from the ceiling.

The room felt eerily cold.

Elch's voice trembled at the unbelievably gruesome spectacle laid before him.

"Th-those are...people?!"

"They probably employed a bunch of different lies to lure travelers to the inn, got them drunk so they couldn't fight back...then brought them down here."

"Wh-why would they do something like this?! Ah—" Suddenly,

Elch remembered wondering how a simple farming village could possess such wealth.

"That's it! They kill travelers and take their money! That's why they seem so rich..."

However—

"That's what I thought at first, but it looks like money wasn't the only thing they were after."

—Shinobu rejected his hypothesis as she stepped into the cellar.

She cast her light on one of the suspended corpses' ankles. It looked to have once been a man but was missing a head and one of its hands.

"Look. See the deep cut on the ankle? You're a hunter, so you know what that means."

The question sent a chill up Elch's spine. He did. Cut off the head. Slice through the vein in the ankle. Hang upside down.

There was no mistaking that process.

"...They've had their blood drained..."

"That's right. And the organs were removed cleanly, so they're definitely being prepared for consumption... This village is a den of murderers, right down to the bone. Literally."

"Bluuurgh!"

Unable to take it anymore, Elch dropped to his knees and ejected the contents of his dinner.

"Yeah, probably better just to get it all out of your system. Guess I beat you to the punch a bit there."

"This is sick... So wait, do you think what they fed us was...?"

"Nah, we're fine there. That was all horse meat."

"H-horse?"

"Remember that abandoned wagon by the inn? It probably belonged to one of these guys. The villagers used its horse to throw us that feast. If they fed us people and scared us off, it'd defeat the whole purpose. Besides, trading the horse flesh it takes to fill a couple bellies for two whole bodies' worth of meat is a pretty good deal."

"Urrrgh…" The idea of using *hyuma* and *byuma* as food filled Elch's throat with bile all over again. How could people even do that? Elch thought back to the smiles the villagers had been wearing all afternoon. They'd seemed like decent people, not barbarians.

Then, it hit him.

As he was thinking about the villagers' faces, he finally realized something. Everyone else had been smiling from beginning to end, but Milinda's expression had wavered for a moment.

Wait, was she…?

Had she been trying to warn them? However, the young man's train of thought was soon interrupted. A shrill, ear-piercing whistle shattered the air.

""_____?!""

As the two of them looked up in confusion, they heard a voice echo down from aboveground: loud, male, and booming.

"Silver Knight Jeanne du Leblanc is here for an inspection! Show yourselves!"

"What's going on?"

"Dunno. Guess we'd better go check it out…!"

After emerging from the inn's cellar, Shinobu and Elch sneaked out the back entrance and looked toward the central plaza's fountain from their concealed spot. A most unusual scene greeted the duo's eyes.

Some dozen-odd armored soldiers were taking the villagers and lining them up. Emelada, her daughter, and the old man who'd introduced them to Shinobu and Elch were among them.

Then…

"ALL HAIL!"

When the conspicuously large soldier shouted at them, the villagers chanted a reply in unison while wearing the same radiant smiles with which they'd greeted Shinobu and Elch.

""""We are grateful for your visit!""""

""""It's been another day of joy and good fortune for us common folk!""""

""""And we owe it all to His Majesty, the Emperor!""""

With the villagers' practiced mantra completed, the red-haired, silver-armored woman who'd been waiting behind the soldiers dismounted from her horse and strode over to them.

She swept her razor-sharp gaze across their lineup.

"Indeed. I am here today to judge whether or not you present in ways befitting subjects of His Grace… Last week I inspected your village itself, and today, my focus shifts to the appearances and smiles of you, its people. Now, straighten those backs!" The order was issued with a dignified tone.

""""Yes! Thank you!""""

The villagers all stood at attention, their backs held unnaturally straight.

The female knight looked each villager over from head to toe, her eagle eyes sparing no detail. After her inspection had gone on for a bit, she ordered those assembled to turn around and repeated the process.

Once the knight was satisfied—

"Very well."

—she would utter a short assessment before moving on to the next in line.

It was like watching someone appraise goods.

"…Oh, huh. I think I get what's going on," Shinobu said.

"You do?"

"I'm just spitballing, but I think this village…no, this whole domain is being *forced* by its lord to keep their towns pretty, their clothes fashionable, and their faces bright."

"B-but what does that even accomplish?"

"I dunno, but…it's not too uncommon for people with absolute power over others to go and do stuff that doesn't really make any sense."

Earth had no shortage of examples. There was a shogun who'd enforced an egotistical set of laws called the Edicts on Compassion for Living Things. Elsewhere, a countess kidnapped serfs and peasant girls, subjected them to sadistic torture, and bathed ecstatically in their blood. Plenty of rulers went and did things that seemed irrational to people with normal dispositions.

Compared to them, that sex maniac Findolph looks like a friendly old man. As Shinobu grinned sarcastically at the thought, a sudden question caught the pair's ears.

"What exactly is this, girl?" The knight's hard question was directed at one person in particular.

"Milinda…!" The girl from the inn where Shinobu and Elch were staying.

"…!"

"The hem of your dress is soiled… One's clothing must be pristine and beautiful, never frayed or stained. Such is the basic requirement for citizens of His Grace's empire. It is my duty to punish those who cannot fulfill such basic requirements."

"Ah… I…"

As the knight solemnly issued her verdict, Milinda's whole body began shaking pitifully as tears rolled down her cheeks.

Her mother, Emelada, quickly moved as though to shield her—

"P-please wait, my lady!"

—and offered the knight a plea.

"A child's failing lies with her parent. Please punish me instead…!"

The woman's reply, "No," was short and final.

"Parent, child, it matters not. Our lord commands that the guilty be punished— You. Prepare her."

"Yes, my lady!"

"Mama! Help me, Mama!"

"Milinda! Please, I beg of you, have mercy…!" Emelada made another desperate petition. However, her words fell on deaf ears.

"Your smile is slipping." The voice of the female knight was like cold steel—utterly devoid of mercy.

"…?!"

"The citizens under His Grace's protection must always smile as proof of their gratitude. Our lord has decreed that as law… I am willing to overlook your fault thus far as that of a concerned parent. However, there will be no second chances. If you persist in your whining and obstruction of justice, I will have the heads of you and your daughter both."

"…"

"Smile." As the knight spoke, the woman moved her hand to the sword at her waist.

If Emelada failed to comply, her life would end in a single slash. Her daughter, Milinda, would be next. As such…Emelada had no choice but to forcibly raise the corners of her mouth into a stiff smile. All the while, the soldiers were binding Milinda.

A brawny one held the poor girl's head still while the others drove a pair of stakes into the ground, wound a rope around them, and used it to bind her legs. Milinda sobbed and tried to flee, but there was only so much a child's strength could accomplish. A soldier with a lash made from a series of leather straps stood behind her.

"Keep the strikes to her buttocks. If you hit a girl that small in the back or the chest, she'd die before you got to the thirtieth lash," the knight commanded.

"Yes, my lady!"

"Now, begin the punishment."

A dry crack echoed through the twilit winter night.

"AHHHHHHHHHHHHHHHHHHHHHHHHHHHHHHHHHHH HH!!!!"

Immediately thereafter, it was joined by a young girl's scream. No matter how much Milinda cried, however, the soldier didn't stop. The lash struck her clothed behind.

"Milinda, be strong! You must endure this!"

"AAAAAAAAAAAAAAAAAAAAAAAGH!!!!"

Her skirt ripped a mere three strikes in, and by the fifth, her skin was broken and raw.

"Th-that's awful…! All that, just 'cause her dress was a little dirty?!" Elch rose to his feet. However, Shinobu grabbed him by the shoulder to restrain the hunter.

"Wait up. What're you doing?"

"I'm gonna save her! I can't just sit here and watch this!"

"Those people were trying to trap us and eat us like livestock, remember?"

"Yeah, but…! But that kid tried to warn me! She tried to tell me to get out of the village!" Elch hadn't heard the end of Milinda's sentence, yet he was sure of it. That's why he wanted to save her. As they were talking about it, though…the screams finally stopped.

"Ahh… Uhh…"

"Milinda?! Milinda! Stay strong…!"

The little thing's knees gave out, and a dark stain began spreading around her groin. Shinobu and Elch both had keen vision and could spot that Milinda's eyes had rolled back and that the girl had lost consciousness. If things continued like this, her life was in danger!

"—! All right, screw this! I don't care what you say; I'm going!" But when Elch tried to stand again, Shinobu grabbed him by the shoulder once more. As he glowered angrily at her, she spoke.

"I get how you feel, El-El, but I have another idea."

Watching Milinda crumple to the ground, the soldier who'd been whipping her stopped.

"Milady, she's passed out..."

Jeanne, the red-headed knight, remained implacable. "...Continue with the prescribed number of lashes."

"Yes, my lady!"

"No, noooooo! Stop, just stop! My daughter's the only thing I have left of my late husband! She's our future. Please stop hitting her!!!!" Emelada's screams grew ever more frantic.

That moment, though, a star-shaped chunk of metal came flying out of the distant thicket and embedded itself in the lash-wielding soldier's hand.

"AAAAARGH!!!!"

"Huh?!"

"What's going on?!"

"All right, all right, that's enough of that. The girl's gonna die if you keep that up, you know." The sudden attack sent a stir through the soldiers. They all turned toward the source of the voice.

It was a girl with peach-blond hair and a long, fluttering skirt. Shinobu Sarutobi, prodigy journalist.

"Who are you?! You don't look like one of the villagers!"

One of the soldiers drew his sword threateningly and prepared to charge Shinobu. However, Jeanne stopped him.

"Stand down."

"My lady?"

"That peculiar star-shaped throwing weapon is a shuriken. It's a tool used by the Yamato ninjas. There's no telling what could happen if you charge in recklessly."

"Ninja?! You mean…she's one of those?!"

"She wasn't just a traveling performer…!"

Hearing the word *ninja* seemed to strike fear into the villagers and soldiers alike. In fact, the only one who seemed unfazed was Jeanne. She strode toward Shinobu.

"I thought all the ninja villages had been burned to the ground, but it seems there was a survivor. Why show yourself to us, though?"

"I told you, didn't I? I wanted to stop you from killing the girl."

"You wanted to save the child? How foolhardy."

"…"

While the red-haired knight was speaking, soldiers moved to surround Shinobu. Once they'd cut off any avenue of escape, Jeanne drew her sword.

"Unlike samurai, ninja are supposed to remain hidden and strike from the shadows. Now that you've shown yourself and let us pin you down, you're powerless."

Shinobu was indeed encircled by swords on all sides. However, it didn't look like she felt cornered in the slightest.

"How 'bout this, lady knight. Wanna make a deal?" Shinobu grinned like the Cheshire cat as she twirled a kunai around on her finger.

"A deal?"

"Yup. You're right. I can't win against this many people when we're out in the open…but I'm taking at least half of you down with me. And you're first on my list."

""""…!""""

"But if you promise not to hurt the girl anymore, I'll come along quietly. Whaddaya say? Not a bad offer, right?"

"…"

Jeanne hesitated, her sword still pointed at the ninja. After a moment, she called to her subordinate holding Milinda's head down.

"Very well. I accept your condition… Release the child."

"Are you sure, my lady?"

"Make it snappy." The soldier did as he was bid. Seeing that, Shinobu tossed her kunai off to the side.

"Thanks kindly."

Now that she was unarmed, the soldiers rushed at her, kicked her to the ground, and stripped her of her freedom. After making sure the iron manacles were secured around Shinobu's wrists, Jeanne gave an order.

"We're going back to Count Blumheart's castle. Bring the ninja."

""""Yes, my lady!""""

Clapped in chains and in the custody of Jeanne, Shinobu was carted off to Castle Blumheart.

A few minutes earlier, back when Shinobu had stopped Elch from rushing out.

"W-wait, you're gonna go?!"

"Yeah. Here, hold on to my phone and ninja tools for me. Oh, and later, let Tsukes know that I got captured on purpose. You know how to use my phone, right?"

"I—I do, but couldn't the two of us just take them out without getting taken prisoner...?"

"No, no, you're thinking about it all wrong. We're on an espionage mission. If I let them catch me, I'll be able to make it all the way into their base without lifting a finger. I can't pass up on an opportunity like that... Oh, don't look so worried. I'll have you know that jailbreaks are my specialty."

This was how they decided Shinobu should allow herself to be captured in order to sneak deep into enemy territory.

Elch, who'd been left alone in the village, helped Emelada carry Milinda back into the inn. The little *byuma*'s wounds were brutal and would likely leave a lifelong scar. Fortunately, though, her breathing eventually stabilized, and she drifted into a quiet slumber. Emelada dropped to her hands and knees, thanking Elch between relieved sobs.

"Oh, thank you, thank you, thank you...! You saved my daughter...!"

"I'd like to thank you, too. I don't know what we would have done if you hadn't been here...," the old man who'd first introduced the mother and daughter added.

However...after seeing what was in the cellar, Elch had no desire to accept their gratitude.

"...I don't need your thanks." The hunter decided to cut right to the chase. "Not when you were planning to kill and eat us."

Emelada's and the old man's faces went pale.

"Wh—?!"

"H-how do you...?!"

"We found the cellar. It made me chuck up my dinner, so I'm nice and sober now."

"...I'm so sorry."

"I don't need your apologies, either. I just want an explanation. Why'd you do it?"

As Elch cut off Emelada's apology—

"...It's a simple thing, really. It was the only way we could survive."

—the old man answered.

"There's nothing else in the town to eat, see."

In a resigned tone, he explained to Elch what had happened to the village. Originally, Coconono Village had made their living harvesting grain. They hadn't been rich by any means but were blessed with fertile land, so they were able to live modest lives free of want. However, once Gustav was granted control over the domain in recognition of his efforts destroying the Yamato Empire, everything went to hell.

The duke ordered that the land was to be made into "a garden befitting His Grace's majesty," decreeing that all the towns and villages in the domain undergo beautification projects. The citizens were forced to rebuild their old houses, repaint them at regular intervals, install glass windows, and wear tailored outfits the likes of which were normally reserved for nobles. All the expenses for these fineries came out of the citizens' pockets, of course.

Such imperatives quickly drained the coffers of the people. Complicating things were the regular inspections by the soldiers. These check-ins meant the commoners couldn't get dirty, preventing any decent fieldwork from getting done. While their expenses increased, their productivity dropped off a cliff. As a result, the people fell into famine and destitution.

Then, to make matters worse, Gustav decided he wanted to build a monument and give it to the emperor to commemorate his conquest of the New World. He immediately commissioned a sixteen-foot-tall solid gold statue of Emperor Lindworm.

However, the heavy taxes its construction demanded would

have been crippling in the best of times and marked the final nail in the coffins of the commoners. The people of Coconono were no exception.

"At that rate, the only fate that awaited us was death by starvation. But the mayor gave us an order… He told us to ply travelers with alcohol, offer them lodging, kill them, strip them of their possessions…and partake of their flesh."

"…!" Elch was struck speechless by Gustav's atrocious governance. No matter how hard the commoners worked, there was no way they could pay for a gold statue, cosmetic upkeep on their villages, glass windows, and fountains while still having enough to feed themselves. The situation was impossible no matter how you looked at it. And yet…

No matter how bad you have it, there are still things you just can't do…! The sins the village had committed were utterly inhuman. They were the acts of savage beasts who had cast aside morals and reason.

"Lemme see this mayor of yours! I need to give that jackass a piece of my mind!"

"…That's not possible."

"Oh yeah?! And why not?!" As Elch snapped at him, the old man replied in an exhausted tone.

"The mayor…my son—Emelada's husband…left us those instructions in his will. As penance for the savagery he'd suggested, he offered up his flesh as the first of our new meals…"

"…!" Elch was stunned quiet yet again. How must Emelada and the others have felt eating his body to prolong their own lives? Just thinking about it left the hunter from Elm at a loss for words. The silence was broken by the old man's weeping.

"Why…? Why did this happen to us…? Our houses were run-down, our clothes were shabby, and we were always covered in dirt…but sharing simple meals with our families was all the happiness we needed… Just that was enough to make us joyous from the bottom of our hearts. But now…not even our smiles are our own…"

There was nothing to smile about, no happiness to be found. Yet they'd been forced to spend their days beaming. It had stretched the old man's spirit to its limit.

That was why—

"I'm just…so tired…"

"Father!"

—the old man pulled a dagger from his coat pocket and stabbed himself through the neck.

Or rather, he tried to. Elch had grabbed it by the blade in the nick of time.

"…Please don't stop me. Just let me die."

"That's not gonna happen."

"…You would have me keep suffering…?" The old man spat the words like a curse. Elch responded by shaking his head.

"That's not it. I just don't want you giving those bastards your life on top of everything else!"

Once again, it became clear to Elch how important their battle was. They needed to change the world. The continued existence of a world that let things like this keep happening was unforgivable. Thus, the young hunter swore an oath to the old man and all the other citizens of this domain.

"I can't do much about all the stuff you've lost…but I swear, we're gonna help you get your smiles back! That's what we're standing up and fighting for…!"

Evening turned to night.

Jeanne had taken the captured Shinobu Sarutobi to the castle of

Count Blumheart, the man Lord Gustav had entrusted with managing many of the domain's towns and villages, including Coconono.

At the moment, Shinobu was in the castle's underground dungeon, stripped down to her underwear and chained to the wall by her wrists. Likely, her cell doubled as an interrogation room. Other than the ninja, it was home to a number of ghastly objects.

Whoa, they've got a Spanish donkey? I've never seen one in person before. Looks pretttty nasty. And is that one a scavenger's daughter? I think so.

"Heh-heh. Scared?"

"Get ready, 'cause we're gonna be using all of them."

The two guards outside the cell cast vulgar gazes up and down Shinobu's body. The girl ignored them and began planning.

Now then, what to do?

It was a shame they hadn't taken her to the actual lord's castle, but there was still probably valuable information she could get here. The question was, how best to go about it? If Shinobu wanted to, she could force her way out whenever she pleased…but in doing so, her captors would go on high alert, making it harder to scour the castle for intel.

The journalist decided it would be better to lie low and wait for a chance to stage a stealthier breakout. After which, Shinobu could sneak into the count's chambers and take him hostage. Pumping that man for the information she needed on Gustav would probably be the easiest way to go.

Suddenly, something interrupted the young woman's train of thought. She could hear the door leading out of the dungeon opening, and her jailer, Jeanne, entered with a bespectacled *byuma* maid in tow. The maid carried a large wooden box.

"Elaine, set the tools down over there."

"Ah, yes, milady…! There we are." A loud, metal clang rang out from inside the container as the maid set it down. Within were pliers, a hammer, a saw, and a variety of other normal-looking tools. However, all of them were covered in dark red rust.

Shinobu could tell they hadn't been used to build anything. These were implements for taking people apart.

I figured she wouldn't be coming around today 'cause of how late it is, but I guess she's pulling overtime. Lady cares about her job, I'll give her that. I would've preferred she didn't, but oh well.

However, even in the face of all those cruel utensils, Shinobu didn't flinch. The girl was no normal high schooler. She was an honest-to-god *kunoichi* and a member of a proud line that stretched all the way back to the Sengoku period. Shinobu had trained to resist any conceivable form of torture. Such experience had given the girl confidence. Tools of that caliber had no chance of breaking her.

Guess I just gotta grit my teeth and endure it for now, huh.

There seemed no urgency to act until the damage to her body looked like it might impact her ability to break out. As Shinobu settled on her strategy, the two guards opened her cell.

"Hee-hee, want us to get started right away?"

"This is gonna be good."

However, Jeanne gave them a new order.

"You two, outside."

"Huh? B-but, Captain, won't it be dangerous with just you?!"

"I'm a woman, too, you know. Even I have my qualms about letting men leer at a lady in agony."

"She's the enemy. You don't need to show her mercy like that…"

"Don't mistake this for what it isn't. I find it objectionable, nothing more. Now leave…before I make you." With that, Jeanne drew the silvery metal whip from her waist and cracked it by the guards' feet. The strike drew fractures in the stone brick floor.

"Eep!"

"Y-yes, my lady! Please, take your time!"

The guards shrieked and noisily clambered up the stairs leading out of the dungeon. Shinobu grinned sarcastically at Jeanne's decision.

"I might not look like I'm in much of a position to be saying this, but aren't you taking this ninja a bit too lightly?"

"Not in the slightest," the knight replied with a faint smile as she approached Shinobu…

…and unfastened the restraints around her wrists.

"Huh?"

Jeanne hadn't just unlocked one side but both of them. There was nothing binding the young *kunoichi*-journalist anymore. Topping off this unusual turn of events, Jeanne even knelt before Shinobu and offered her a bow.

"You have my deepest thanks for saving that girl. You do your Yamato brethren proud."

"…Beg your pardon?"

Wait, what gives? Shinobu was unable to hide her confusion at the thoroughly unexpected conclusion to her imprisonment.

As she gawked—

"Elaine?"

"Ah, yes, right away, ma'am."

—the knight ordered Elaine to give Shinobu all her clothes and equipment back from where they'd been concealed, beneath the torture implements.

"It's winter, so if you stay like that too long, you'll catch a cold. I believe these belong to you."

"…Wait, what's going on right now?" Shinobu asked, still totally baffled.

Jeanne rose and clenched her fist in front of her chest.

*　　*　　*

"Allow me to introduce myself once more. I am Jeanne du Leblanc, a Silver Knight in service to the empire and to Count Blumheart. I am also a member of the Blue Brigade, an organization that fears for the future of the Gustav domain. You, who traveled far from Yamato to infiltrate this land, and we of the Blue Brigade share a common enemy—the Fastidious Duke, Oslo el Gustav.

"It is said that 'the enemy of my enemy is my friend.' Ninja of Yamato, won't you lend us your dauntless courage that we might save the suffering people of this land?"

CHAPTER 5

🔱 Crimson Night 🔱

"It's magnificent! Its beauty stirs my very soul!"

The Gustav domain was home to the Office of the Warden of the North. There, enshrined in the palace, was a gold statue glimmering beautifully in the bright torchlight. A majestic middle-aged man with long black hair and an impressive beard—Oslo el Gustav, the Fastidious Duke—shed tears of joy as he beheld the sight of the monument.

He sighed feverishly as he spoke. "Immortalizing His Grace in bronze or stone? That would be inexcusable. But a statue of pure gold is just the thing to cement the emperor's authority in the minds of the people..."

"I've already talked to Count Perscheid about having it placed in the imperial capital's central gardens, milord. As soon as we transport it there, it'll be installed in the middle of the main fountain. If it pleases you, I have a concept sketch here."

As Gustav trembled on his knees before the statue, his secretary—a short, older man named Oscar—stepped into the shadow Gustav cast in the light of the flame and gave his report in a high, nasally voice. The man handed his lord a rolled-up piece of parchment.

Gustav unfurled it and nodded in satisfaction. "Marvelous work.

Count Perscheid is hailed as the most stylish man in the empire, so I knew I could count on him... Have the means of transport been arranged?"

"Yes, milord. As you know, a statue of pure gold is too heavy for horses, cattle, or dragons to pull. I was thinking that we might use elephants."

"What's an 'elephant'?"

"A beast we've been importing alongside the slaves from the New World. They used to live in the southern parts of the empire as well but were wiped out due to the high demand for their ivory. Their bodies are massive, and they boast such strength that some New World natives even ride them into battle. A team of four such creatures should be sufficient to carry the statue to the capital."

"...So feral horses?"

Gustav wasn't exactly pleased at having creatures like that be the ones to transport the physical symbol of his loyalty. At the same time, however, it seemed somewhat fitting to have the statue extolling the emperor's authority carried by beasts belonging to the tribes the emperor himself was in the process of subjugating. The two contradictory thoughts clashed within the Fastidious Duke, but he eventually gave his verdict.

"Very well. However, I place little faith in those savage creatures. I want a troop guarding the statue during transport, and I demand their utmost vigilance. If it suffers so much as a single scratch, every one of those soldiers and their families are to be executed... Am I understood?"

"Absolutely, milord. I will be sure to impress upon them the gravity of their task."

"Hmph. One other thing, Oscar."

"Yes, milord?"

Gustav had called out to his manservant as the latter was preparing to leave. The duke spoke in the same voice he might use to demand a glass of water.

"I hereby commission four more identical statues, one to be installed in each of the empire's cardinal wards. Begin collecting the gold at once." However, the man's request was downright insane.

"Wh—?! F-four more statues, a-all of pure gold, milord?!"

"For the time being. When all is said and done, I aim to have one in every domain in the empire so as to remind the commoners who it is that they serve."

Oscar's face went pale as sweat began gushing out of pores he didn't even know he had.

"N-not gilded, but…solid gold?!"

"Naturally. I will not stand for gilding or other such deception when it comes to the manifestation of my undying loyalty! Or, perhaps, are you suggesting that my devotion itself is gilded, merely surface deep?" As Gustav glowered at him, Oscar instinctively dropped to one knee and bowed.

"H-h-h-heavens no, milord! I—I know full well that your loyalty to His Grace is beyond reproach. H-however, i-if I might be candid… This single gold statue has already put a great burden on the people. I've heard tell that no shortage of them have even been forced to kill and eat their families and travelers to stave off starvation. Should we ask them to produce the funds for four more, well…"

"They'll starve to death, is that it?"

"Y-yes, milord…!"

"Then so be it."

"What?!"

Oscar's eyes went wide. That wasn't the reaction he'd expected.

However, Gustav didn't pay Oscar's surprise the slightest bit of attention. He merely gazed reverently at the statue as he spoke.

"Knights demonstrate their fidelity through martial feats. Nobles, by properly tending to their lands. How, then, are peasants meant to show their loyalty? They have no valor. No wisdom. What minimal gesture can those base creatures make in hopes of showing their devotion?

"There is but one answer: to die for His Grace."

"Wha...?!"

"It's for his sake that they must wear fineries and keep their towns resplendent despite their poverty. Proper expression of gratitude toward the emperor demands that they must wear perpetual smiles despite their misery. That is how the peasantry must comport themselves. The fact that it's wrung from their bodies is what gives the statue's gold its meaning."

As far as Gustav was concerned, gold was little more than lumps of glittering clay. It had no intrinsic difference from inferior materials like bronze and stone. Normally, it would have no right bearing the emperor's form. However, the gold he had used for the statue was no ordinary metal. It had been metaphorically scraped off the peasants' bones, making it the crystallization of their lifeblood.

"This statue is imbued with the devotion of all who dwell within my lands. That is why it's able to serve as a symbol of my loyalty to His Grace! Do you understand now, Oscar?"

Gustav's black gaze drifted toward the servant. Oscar quivered internally. There was no hint of sycophancy, vanity, or self-interest in Gustav's obsidian eyes. The only thing glimmering in their depths was a nigh-boyish sense of unconditional devotion to the emperor.

"It is as you say, milord..." As he acquiesced out of fear, Oscar found his convictions reaffirmed.

...*The man's loyalty is unquestionable. Duke Gustav doesn't have a selfish bone in his body. Just an unflagging willingness to give his all for the emperor. Beautifying the domain, building the gold statue... It's all solely for His Majesty's sake. If His Grace told him to die, Gustav would surely kill himself with a smile on his face.*

Between the duke's mentality and his steadfast devotion, none could be better described as *heroic* than he.

But...as a leader, he's the greatest fool there is!

If things continued as they were, the Gustav domain would be in ruins in the next few years. With their tax base eviscerated, the nobles would be unable to maintain their lifestyle. If that man remained in charge any longer, everyone would be ruined. Gustav's grotesque devotion would be the death of commoners and nobles alike.

We of the Blue Brigade need to carry out our plan, and soon... But to do that, we must have a way to deal with the Treasure Spear. As long as it's converged, trying to destroy it is futile. If only there were some way...

As Oscar contemplated his secret treachery, a voice stirred him from his reverie.

"Now, something else concerns me, Oscar." Gustav went ahead and changed the subject.

Terrified that he'd been found out, Oscar piped up with a shrill, startled "Yes, milord?!"

Fortunately for him, though—

"Has the rebellion in Findolph been suppressed yet?"

—what Gustav wanted to talk about had nothing to do with his secretary's secret.

Oh, it's just that... Oscar breathed an internal sigh of relief as he gave his answer.

"We've successfully coordinated with Marquises Buchwald and Archride, milord. Supplies and provisions are being brought to the

Le Luk Mountain Range checkpoint as we speak, and our troops are amassing in the foothills. Come spring, the military roads will be usable, and a hundred thousand of our troops will march on Dormundt and purge every last traitor from its walls."

They were making full use of the time before the war started to get their supply lines up and running. Marquis Archride had been renowned as a masterful general during the last emperor's rule, and it was clear why. Oscar then went on, laying out their troops' movements while praising Archride for his superb leadership of the domain's unified forces. Or, rather, that's what the servant tried to do.

However…

"Perhaps I misheard you."

At Gustav's interjection, Oscar went silent. The Fastidious Duke's statement and the tone in which he made it sent a chill down the man's spine. Gustav's voice was a blade of ice. Oscar could practically feel the air around him freeze, crack, and shatter into tiny fragments. The secretive conspirator had a nasty feeling about this.

"…'Come spring'? 'Come spring,' you said? You mean to tell me that Buchwald and Archride have yet to act? It's been over a month since I ordered the subjugating army to deploy! Those vermin still trample upon one of our emperor's holy domains…

"…AND WE ALLOW THEM TO RUN RAMPANT?!?!?!"

"Yeeeeeeeeeeeeek!!!!" Oscar's fears had been instantly confirmed.

Gustav bellowed in rage, lashing out around himself as he clawed at his scalp and ripped out his hair. "Such…such utter disgrace! Such utter ineptitude! His Grace entrusted me with these northern lands! How could I let those insects fester for an entire month?! AaaaaaaaaaAAAAAARRRRGGGGHHHH!!!!"

When his shriek reached its climax, he knelt before the gold statue, placed his hands on the ground…

…and smashed his head into the hard floor.

"M-milord?!"

"O-one thousand apologies, Your Graaaaaace! I'm an inept fool! H-how can I ever atone for this?! Grrrr…GRAAAAAAAAAAAH!!!!"

It wasn't just once, either. In a display of utter mercilessness, Gustav brought his forehead to bear on the stone floor over and over again as he wailed. Even as his skin tore and blood pooled on the ground, he refused to stop.

"Eep…" Oscar could no longer begin to comprehend Gustav's behavior, and when someone was faced with something outside their ability to understand, their only option was to fear it. The servant's heart froze. All he could do was cower in silence as he watched his deranged master.

Eventually, Gustav stopped slamming his head and called for his manservant. "…Oscar."

"Y-yes, milord!"

"Bring me Rage Soleil from my bedchamber…"

Oscar found himself unable to hide his shock.

"Y-you really mean to use the Treasure Spear now…?!"

"ARE YOU DEAF, YOU IMBECILE?! I SAID TO BRING IT HERE!!!!"

"R-right away, milord!"

The sheer menace of the duke's bloodstained face and furious howling sent Oscar dashing over to Gustav's nearby bedchamber.

Enshrined almost reverently on a pedestal at the back of the room was a pulsating red spear. That was the true form of Gustav's legendary so-called Heavenly Fire.

"Rage Soleil."

For five long years, Gustav had spent five hours each day chanting incantations before a raging flame in order to complete his war magic. It was his ultimate trump card.

Oscar lifted the spear, pedestal and all. The weapon was formed from a convergence of bound, materialized blaze spirits, so it was as hot as burning iron. For a normal person, touching it was out of the question. Making sure to hold it by the pedestal, the servant returned to his lord. Finally, he knelt before Gustav, who was waiting by the gold statue.

"Milord, if I—"

"Out of the way!" Gustav didn't hesitate for a moment before grabbing the spear with his bare hands and kicking Oscar aside. The little man let out a "Gyah!" as the Fastidious Duke shoved past him and made for the palace's highest spire.

I was an idiot for trusting the likes of Buchwald and Archride! Worthless incompetents, the lot of them! They're toxic parasites leeching off of the empire, nothing more...!

Gustav made his way up the spire's spiral staircase, paying no heed to the heat searing his flesh down to the bone. Eventually, the man reached the tower's apex. Standing before a large golden bell, the duke glared off into the northern sky.

He was staring at the land past the horizon. Gustav was certain something was squirming just beyond his view. Vermin, running rampant in His Grace's territory, encroaching on Findolph and devouring it all! It was unacceptable. Utterly unforgivable. There was only one natural recourse in the duke's mind…

Now is the time to unleash my fury—my Rage Soleil!

"HRAAAAAAAAAAAAAAAAAAAAAAAAAAAAAAAA AGH…!"

The moment Gustav unleashed the seal on his spear-shaped war magic, he used every ounce of his spiritual energy to bind the wind spirits dwelling in the atmosphere. From the spirits, a green aura began welling up. Gustav's curse bound them, imbuing the spear with the power of flight. Such was the energy it needed to cross seas and mountains, piercing through clouds on its journey to strike down its master's hideous enemies.

With the deadly magic prepared—

"THEY WILL LEARN JUST HOW HOT MY WRATH BURNS!!!!"

—Oslo el Gustav hurled the spear into the northern sky toward Dormundt.

As the snow laid thick atop the ground, a thunderous gust of wind cleaved through the cloudy night. Lyrule heard a strange voice call to her in a dream.

"Please, wake up…"

Jade-green flecks of light floated up through the darkness of her unconscious mind, drifting in a snowflake-like pattern. That was where the sound originated. It was the voice of a woman.

The noise wasn't hitting her eardrums but rather echoing directly in her brain.

"A crisis...befalls the Seven Heroes... A crisis...is imminent..."

"The Seven Heroes." Lyrule didn't understand what that meant, but she knew it referred to her friends from Earth. For some reason, she was certain of it. Like she'd known it from the very beginning.

The voice continued.

"They require...your power... Please...you have to...guide them..."

It was pleading with the girl.

"—?!"

Quite suddenly, Lyrule sprang up from the world of dreams. Her breath was ragged. She placed a hand on her chest.

"What...was that, just now...?" The young woman didn't know. She couldn't even begin to comprehend it. Yet, curiously, Lyrule was filled with certainty.

Something terrible was about to happen to her friends.

I'm scared... The blond girl's body trembled. What in the world was happening to her? Lyrule didn't know, and it terrified her.

However, as if to drive the point home—

"...Help..."

"...?!"

—a heartbroken voice echoed through her ears.

It wasn't the woman from the dream but rather...children. Thousands of them, crying out in unison. Lyrule leaped out of her bed and threw open her window.

"Please...help us..."

It was more than the imagination of a sleepy mind. The girl could really hear them. Their voices were quieter than the sound of snow falling, yet still their cries reached Lyrule. She could hear them calling out from above the snow-laden clouds.

Meanwhile—

"*This is be〜ry baaaaaaaad!!!!*"

In Ringo Oohoshi's lab in the newly established Manufacturing District, Bearabbit rose from sleep mode with a shout.

"Bearabbit?!" Ringo sat up, wondering what had the AI so alarmed all of a sudden.

The artificial creature broadcast the situation through the myriad communication terminals to which he was linked.

"*This is an emergency notification to all devices! Altitude, twenty thousand feet! Distance, one hundred and twenty-five miles away! A projectile has been located approaching Dormundt from the south-southeast! Enacting emergency protocols!*"

"…! Open all air-defense missile pods! Prepare to intercept!"

"*Pawger that!*" Bearabbit set to immediately carrying out Ringo's instructions. As the center of the air-defense system's network, he opened the missile pods' anti-snow roofs and readied them to fire. Then…

"*Ringo.*"

The inventor had quickly opened up her Bearabbit-synched laptop, and its communication app initialized. A call was coming from Tsukasa, who'd been leading a staff meeting over in Dormundt proper.

"Oh, um, Tsukasa! I, uh…"

"*I got the gist of the situation from the emergency notification just now. Do we know what the bogey is yet?*"

"From what the sonar analysis is telling us, I think it's a spear."

"Based on its current trajectory and bearing, we've got a point of origin! It came from the Gustav domain!"

"A-at this rate, it's going to hit...r-right in the middle of Dormundt!"

"That's clearly no ordinary spear. Odds are it's Oslo el Gustav's infamous Heavenly Fire. Do whatever it takes to shoot it down, Ringo."

The scientific genius accepted the order without hesitation. "Leave it...to us! Bearabbit! The air-defense counterattack is ready, right?!"

"Fur sure!" Bearabbit sent the command to have one of their four missile pods launch its entire salvo.

Smoke burst from the cylindrical pod as its twenty miniature missiles blasted off into the snowy sky. Each one hurtled toward the crimson shooting star that had just penetrated the cloud line over Dormundt.

Flowers of red flame blossomed in the cold winter sky. Twenty massive blossoms. A moment later, the sounds of the explosion rocked the city. Thanks to the unparalleled accuracy of Bearabbit's guidance, each missile had struck true.

However...

The AI was monitoring the situation via radar, so he noticed the abnormality before all the eyesight-reliant humans. Despite how heavily it had just been bombed, the projectile was undamaged.

"N-no good! That whole bearrage had no effect?!"

"But...why...?!" Ringo's eyes swam; she couldn't believe it. From the other end of the call, Tsukasa offered her a possible explanation.

"It must be guarded by some kind of magic..."

"If it took that hit without a scratch, then shooting it down is going to be nigh impawsible."

"But then...what can we do...?"

Ringo flew into a tizzy at the unexpected turn of events. However, Tsukasa was different. The young prime minister was the type to be prepared for each and every eventuality he could conceive of. Cool and collected, he moved on to their next option.

"...*Ringo, was there any change in the spear's trajectory and landing site before and after our counterstrike?*"

"Ah, um, h-hold on a second... I'll run the numbers!" The scientist did as requested and recalculated the spear's flight path. The results...gave her a ray of hope.

"It shifted...to the High-End Residential District in the southwest...!"

"*If we can't destroy it, maybe we can push it away. New plan: I need you to use the missiles to divert the spear outside the city. The farther, the better.*"

Despite the new plan, Ringo faltered. "W-will we be okay...?" She was clearly worried. Even without her saying specifically what she was concerned about, Tsukasa could tell.

She was scared that even if they managed to knock the spear off its initial target, they might still get swallowed in the ensuing destruction. Thankfully, Tsukasa had already come up with an answer to that problem.

"*Gustav's Heavenly Fire posed a significant threat to us, so I've spent quite a bit of my free time over the past month researching it. We're a good distance from the battlefield he fought the Yamato Empire on, so it's been difficult to track down accurate accounts. From the size of the base he destroyed, the time it took for the base to fall, and the consistencies between various retellings of the story, though, it appears Heavenly Fire is less like an explosive and more like a firebomb. If we don't take the hit head-on, we shouldn't be in much danger. Do it.*"

Tsukasa hadn't just spent the past month wallowing in helplessness. The white-haired boy had busied himself taking in all the information he possibly could and used it to discern their enigmatic foe's true nature. Armed with such knowledge, the young man spoke very assuredly.

Despite being of another world—with little knowledge about magic—Tsukasa had a pretty good handle on Rage Soleil's specifics. Now that she knew about the research and investigation backing up Tsukasa's confidence, Ringo was satisfied.

"Got...it! Bearabbit, let's use the missiles to knock the spear's angle down...so it lands in the sea outside the city!"

"Pawger that!" Bearabbit followed Ringo's instructions and activated the second missile pod. After he guided the projectiles' trajectory so as to strike the spear's raised head from above, they made impact.

The plan was flawless.

Rage Soleil itself was composed of the blaze spirits Gustav had spent five years binding together. Shallow attacks like those of the missiles couldn't so much as scratch it. However, the magic Gustav was using to make it fly wasn't nearly so powerful.

Destroying the spear may not have been possible, but when the duke had thrown it, all he'd been able to enchant it with was tactical magic. Using missiles to mess with its propulsion was definitely feasible. Its projected landing site crept farther and farther away from the city's center and moved ever closer to the sea outside the city.

With the third missile pod, they were able to shift it all the way to the city's outskirts. All that was left was the fourth and final barrage.

Once they launched the missiles from the High-End Residential District's pod, they'd be able to make the spear crash into the sea. Ringo breathed a sigh of relief, but it proved to be short-lived.

"Good stuff! Now, the furth pod should seal the—what?!"

Suddenly, Bearabbit let out an alarmed cry.

"What's wrong?!"

"The launch mechanism in the High-End Residential District's missile pod isn't responding! We can't launch the missiles!"

"You're kidding?!" Ringo tried frantically to access the fourth pod from her computer and force-start the launch sequence. However, all she got for her troubles was a big error message informing her that there was an analog equipment failure.

"Analog error? How?! Did some snow get in and damage the system?!"

"It's too late! The spear's making impact!"

"Ah! Tsukasa, run—!"

"GET DOWN!!!!"

"_____?!"

Ringo's body reacted to Tsukasa's bellow faster than her mind did. She threw herself to the ground. The next moment, a red flash of light engulfed the city.

After crossing seas and mountains, Rage Soleil finally crashed in Dormundt. The magic spear landed in the High-End Residential District's park, a hot spot for social gatherings.

On impact, the already-luminous weapon let out its largest flash of light yet. The crimson glare was so intense, it was visible all the way from the Former-Commoners' Residential District. After the light, the spear emitted a bright-red blast of flame. It instantly spread three hundred feet in each direction before spiraling up into the air. All in the city wondered what was happening.

Seeing the light, feeling the heat, and hearing the screams of those caught up in the inferno snapped the High-End Residential District's residents back to their senses. They fled to escape the terrible magic's radius.

That was when it appeared.

As the pillar of flame rose into the sky, it took on the shape of a person. The fires writhed as though possessing a will of their own, molding themselves into the form of a man's torso. The crackling blaze became the visage of an austere man with long hair and a beard.

"I-i-it's hiiiiiim!"

Some of the district's nobles trembled as they stared into the fiery face. They had seen its like before. Eventually, the crimson man's mouth moved to speak. Its words blew through the whole of Dormundt like a tempestuous wind.

"I am His Grace's loyal knight. I am Oslo el Gustav. I speak now to the insects defiling His Grace's sacred garden and to those foolish enough to ally with them.

"Know now that there is nowhere in these northern lands I protect for the likes of you to nest. The flames of my rage…shall burn your very souls to dust!"

And with that, the fiery figure raised its molten arms to the heavens and spoke the incantation.

"RAGE SOLEIL!"

That moment, the figure crumbled from the base up…and released a tidal wave of awesome fire.

In the blink of an eye, the flood consumed half the district. And the fires didn't stop spreading there. Plants, buildings, and people were all burned away indiscriminately.

"Ahhhhhh!"

"Wh-what's going on?!"

"Eeeeeeeeeeeek!

"It's Duke Gustav's Heavenly Fire! We're doomed!"

Engulfed in flame, the High-End Residential District looked like hell on earth. Crimson tongues licked at the residences' beautifully tiled walls, consuming them along with the lustrous blue rooftops that had served as a symbol of the nobles' statuses. However, what really made the landscape seem hellish were the screams of its residents.

Some people had to flee their burning houses with only the clothes on their backs. Others greedily tried making off with their riches in tow only to be swallowed by the inferno. More still had already been reduced to human-shaped mounds of charcoal.

Nobles and their employees fled every which way, trying desperately to escape the waking nightmare. Among them were the three young nobles who'd refused to submit to the Seven Luminaries and had been plotting to collude with Marquis Archride and commit acts of terrorism.

"Hey, Kyle! What's going on?!"

"How the hell should I know?!"

"Did I just hear that thing say 'Oslo el Gustav'?!"

"D-don't be a dumbass! He'd never attack while we nobles are still in the city! Wh—?!"

That's when the three saw it; a large object was falling toward them from above. By the time they'd spotted it, there was nothing they could have done. A burning home's chimney had crumbled at its base and was toppling toward the three of them.

Responding to imminent danger required training to develop the reflexes needed for proper evasion. Most folk were like deer. No matter how nimble they were, these people would freeze up when faced with an onrushing car. The three would-be-terrorist-nobles were no exception. They went stock-still. Not even screams escaped their mouths.

However—

"Hyaaaaaah!"

—something stopped the crumbling mass of brick the moment before it could crush them.

A man rushed toward them like a gust of wind, then swung his crude iron slab of sword and smashed the chimney away. The stone column must have weighed hundreds of pounds, yet this man had been able to repel it with brute strength alone.

"Hey, it's Niersbach and co. You kids all right?"

"Y-you're that..."

Their savor was familiar to all three of the nobles. That one-eyed *byuma* with droopy dog ears had once served as Dormundt's captain of the guard. However, out of lust for authority, he'd abandoned his pride, betrayed his country, and taken a job as commander of the Order of the Seven Luminaries. At least, that was how the nobles evaluated the ex-Silver Knight, Zest Bernard.

The man in question had responded to the crisis quickly. Having shed their armor, he and his soldiers had come running to help.

"Is everyone all right?"

Tsukasa turned his gaze away from the window where he'd just watched the blazing figure vanish and now turned toward the government officials gathered in the conference room.

Right before the spear landed, they'd reflexively thrown themselves to the ground at Tsukasa's instruction. Now, upon hearing his question, they gingerly rose back to their feet. Fortunately, none of them were injured. The municipal office was fairly close to the city's center, a fair distance from Rage Soleil's impact site over by the outer perimeter.

That was not to say that the assembled politicians were of sound mind after the attack. Given their expressions, many of them were clearly panicking over the current state of emergency.

"Mr. Tsukasa! Wh-what's going on…?!"

"It appears the High-End Residential District was hit by a spear-like projectile originating from the Gustav domain. The empire has clearly launched some manner of magical attack against us."

"B-but that must be…!"

"C-could it really be the Fastidious Duke's infamous Heavenly Fire?!"

"The attack he used in the war against Yamato to destroy their massive base in a single night?!"

Winter was only half over, so the officials were shaken by Tsukasa's declaration.

"Mr. Tsukasa, wh-what do we do?!"

"The fire's gonna be here any minute now! We gotta get outta here!"

"B-but not all the residents managed to get out yet…!"

However, right as the officials started getting restless—

"Remaaaaaain caaaaaalm!"

—a booming voice filled the air.

It was so loud it was likely heard through all of Dormundt.

Akatsuki's voice echoed from the megaphones installed throughout the city.

"This is Akatsuki, God of the Seven Luminaries! Right now, I'm speaking directly into your minds! Employees and former nobles of the High-End Residential District, listen well!

"As I'm sure you're aware, the empire has launched an underhanded attack against Dormundt! They wanted to destroy our fair city and were happy to let you former nobles burn along with it! But worry not! We of the Seven Luminaries will not forsake you!

"Our soldiers are heading your way to carry out rescue operations! Follow their instructions so you can get to safety quickly! If any of you are trapped inside burning buildings, lean out a window and wave your hands so they can find you! We won't leave a single man, woman, or child behind! I repeat—"

At the moment, he was soaring above the burning district, making a show of himself and casting his voice to encourage its evacuating residents. All the while, the unarmored soldiers were following Zest's orders, directing the fleeing civilians toward shelter and rescuing people from burning buildings.

The fire had barely even started, yet their efforts were already well under way. None of them had panicked or hesitated for a moment. However, that was to be expected. Everything they were doing had been laid out well ahead of time.

"That's right! Item three, clause two in the *Emergency Manual*!" It was Mayor Heiseraat who realized.

"Ah, I see you've remembered." Tsukasa nodded to indicate that the man was right.

The *Emergency Manual* was exactly what its name suggested—it was a document detailing what each person in the city needed to do in the event of one of any number of dire situations. Having a large-scale fire break out in the High-End Residential District was item three, clause two of that manual.

Tsukasa Mikogami knew all too well that he wasn't omnipotent. He couldn't know what the future held. This was why he made a plan for every conceivable eventuality before it happened.

"At this stage, I have no direct orders for you all. You already know what you need to do in situations like this, and you have the manpower and tools to carry it out. Once I'm gone, you all will be responsible for protecting this city for many years to come... Remain calm and collected; mindfully do what needs to be done." To demonstrate that there was no need to panic, Tsukasa leisurely positioned himself on the sofa.

With a rare smile—

"It'll be okay. You can do this."

—he indicated to the officials his wholehearted confidence in them.

The white-haired boy's demeanor demonstrated something to the gathered bureaucrats. What drove Tsukasa to work so unreasonably hard all the time wasn't a mere addiction to the job. Rather, it was so he could act calmly in times of crisis. Simply put, it was so Tsukasa could get enough done ahead of time to give everyone else some room to breathe when the time came. Such dedication touched the hearts of those he worked alongside.

""""Yes, sir!"""" The officials responded confidently, then got busy performing their individual tasks.

One of them contacted companies around the city and made arrangements to have blankets delivered to those who'd lost their homes in the fire. Another organized the office employees and began moving key documents off-site. A third reached out to the prodigy doctor, Keine Kanzaki, and coordinated the construction of a treatment camp for the injured.

Once they'd started, each acted with speed and precision. The fact that they could do so was a large part of why they were there. After all, part of a politician's job was to surround themselves with capable staff. Even without Tsukasa lifting a finger, the people were still in good hands.

Even so, I hadn't expected the fire to be quite so ferocious. Tsukasa looked out a shattered window. The blaze had already nearly made its way to his office.

At that rate, the High-End Residential District was going to be completely engulfed, and the fire would spread to the neighboring Port and Former-Commoners' Residential Districts as well. Dormundt was a symbol of the notion of equality that had finally taken root in that world. Tsukasa wasn't about to let it get burned to the ground. He couldn't. The billions of lives yet to enter this world depended on it.

"…It's me." To that end, Tsukasa picked up his phone and got another ball rolling.

After Zest smashed the falling chimney aside, a young *byuma* noble, Kyle, shot him a scathing glare. "You're that traitorous knight who sold out your country to rebels to amass status for yourself. What are you doing saving a bunch of imperial nobles like us?!"

Kyle's one-eyed savior lowered his crude greatsword and let out a small sigh. "…C'mon, li'l Niersbach. Enough of that, already." The old dog-eared soldier grinned sarcastically.

"What?!"

"You kids have it in your heads that you're imperial nobles, so no matter what, the empire's gonna swoop in and save you. But the Fastidious Duke ain't half that kind. You couldn't protect the territory you were entrusted with, and in his eyes, that means you're dead. Look around you; this should be proof enough."

"..."

"Survival of the fittest, remember? That's the empire's policy, and at the end of the day, commoners and nobles are no different from them in that respect. You live when the people above you allow it, and you die like worms when your betters demand it."

"Well, no shit...! That's our empire's golden rule!"

"Well then, you'd better go throw yourselves into Duke Gustav's angry flames, eh? As law-abiding nobles of the realm, ain't that your duty now?"

"Rgh...! Th-that's..." Kyle was at a loss for a response. After all, nobody wanted to die to satisfy another's rage. However, imperial law demanded he submit to that absurdity. Kyle had spent his whole life living under that law. He'd believed it to be the one true absolute. Yet now...

"...But see, the Seven Luminaries are trying to build a world where that ain't the case. A gentler world, where shit like class and bloodlines don't determine how you live and die... Leaving a world like that behind for my daughter? Now that's a dream worth dying for. *That's* the reason I became their commander."

It was never about status for Zest. That wasn't something worth putting his life on the line for. The former knight risked death because he had a dream about something bigger than himself. As Zest finished giving his speech, he turned around.

"I can't begin to imagine how much confusion, pain, and anger you must feel at having to give up the privileges you've spent your whole life enjoying. But...when you start looking at others as equals, you see all sorts of stuff you never even realized you were missing. Do me a favor and remember that."

Zest kept moving. There were still others who needed rescuing. Kyle spat a curse while he watched the old man depart.

"Hey, nobody asked for your help! C'mon, guys, let's get out of here!" The younger *byuma* and his friends ran off to escape the flames.

They, along with the rest of the High-End Residential District's survivors, followed the roadside soldiers' directions and made for the park in the city's central plaza. When they did, though, the blaze ramped up in intensity, as if trying to pursue the fleeing townsfolk. The way the flames were spreading out and engulfing the city, it was like they had a will of their own. However, Tsukasa wasn't about to let that savagery continue.

"Mr. Tsukasa! We're done evacuating the survivors!"

"Good work."

Each division's supervisor had been equipped with a rudimentary comms terminal. After receiving an update from one of them, Tsukasa gave an order to the head of his recently formed counterintelligence division.

"Victor, the evacuation is finished. You're all set to detonate."

"Roger that."

Despite the state of emergency, the reply from the other end was perfunctory and businesslike. A moment later—

"""——?!?!?!"""""

—the sound of several hundred explosions going off rocked the eardrums of every person in the city.

All of Dormundt looked in the direction of the turmoil to try and figure out what was going on. Every building lining the High-End

Residential District's main road had been blasted away without a trace.

Keine, who was in the central plaza treating the injured, immediately understood what had happened. "Ah, I see. By widening the road that divides the city into four sections, he aims to limit the fire's spread."

Aoi nodded as she helped carry survivors too wounded to walk. "Water alone is insufficient to extinguish a conflagration that severe, so that was the only course of action, that it was. Masato, m'lord, I would hardly have thought it possible to acquire such quantities of gunpowder, but it seems I underestimated you."

Masato was directing the flow of supplies, but hearing Aoi's praise, he grinned malevolently. "Oh, I didn't lift a finger. Ol' Saint Nick came over the cold wintry seas to bring them to us as a present."

"Well, I suppose we'll have to thank him, now, won't we?"

"Ah! So Santa exists in this world, too?! A pleasant surprise, that it is!"

Keine chuckled, understanding what Masato was hinting at. Aoi missed the point entirely but was impressed nonetheless.

Suddenly, though—

"...It's not...enough..."

—they saw a familiar blond girl desperately making her way toward them through the crowd.

"Heya, Lyrule. Didja come to help out—" But before Masato could get the "or something?" part out, the good look he got at her stunned him into silence. Even though it was a chilly night in the dead of winter, she was sweating like crazy.

"Hey, whoa, what's with all the sweat?!"

"Oh my, were you burned?!"

Lyrule shook her head at her concerned friends. That wasn't what had happened. She spoke, practically having to wring her voice out of her throat to do so.

"…Widening the road…isn't enough! It won't…be able to stop… Rage Soleil…!"

"Lyrule, what are you—?" Again, before Masato could finish, he was interrupted.

"Don't think for a moment that your petty tricks are enough to escape my wrath!"

Just like before, a gale-force bellow rocked Dormundt.

""""Ahhhhhhhhhhhhh!!!!"""" A great wave of screams rose from the refugee-packed plaza. Cause for such renewed alarm was quickly evident. Having finally burned through the High-End Residential District, the conflagration stopped in front of the explosion-widened main road.

But right when it looked like the blaze was contained…

…thousands of human-shaped flames began crawling out from the inferno.

They slowly rose to their burning feet and began walking forward with their arms outstretched like the blind. With tottering, unstable steps, they crossed the roads toward the Port and Former-Commoners' Residential Districts, grabbing any buildings they could to spread their flames.

Terrifyingly, though, the buildings weren't their only targets. Some even started gradually making their way toward the people gathered in the central plaza.

"The *hell*...?" By Earth logic, it was utterly unfathomable. Even Masato was taken aback.

Gustav cackled scornfully.

"Heh-heh, ah-ha-ha-haaaaaa!!!! Tremble in fear! Cower in terror! For this is the true might of my devotion! This is the might of my war magic, Rage Soleil!

"Once activated, its flames will burn their way to the end of the continent! This nation has nowhere you can hide! Now, die! Die! Atone for your sins with your lives! Perish for the sin of soiling His Grace's sacred lands with your filthy, traitorous feet!!!!"

"E-eeeeek!"

"We're doomed! There's no way we can beat the empire!"

"Ruuuuuuuun!"

Having the flames walk toward them of their own volition was something beyond a nightmare. At such a hellish sight, the people of Dormundt finally knew the height of fear. Frenzied screams echoed from all directions as everyone scrabbled to be the first out of the city. As long as the fire yet burned, trying to calm them would be an exercise in futility.

With a bitter expression on his face, Mayor Heiseraat got on his comms and issued the order. "Attention, all personnel. We're moving to item three, clause four in the *Emergency Manual*. Evacuate the entire city! We're...abandoning Dormundt!"

With Mayor Heiseraat having given the order to evacuate, people in every district fled outside Dormundt's walls.

Terrified as they were of the fantastical flames that had finally swallowed up the High-End Residential District, they rushed to the open gates with only the barest amount of luggage possible. The air was filled with fearful, anxious screams.

Amid all that, Masato and the others remained fixed, steadfast in their positions—and not without reason. As the mayor was giving the evacuation order, Tsukasa had sent them a message.

"I've got one last idea left. Ringo and I are headed your way, so hang tight in the central plaza."

They'd had no problem with the prime minister's new directive. After all, Lyrule had told them pretty much the same thing.

"Fleeing isn't necessary. There's a way to break Rage Soleil."

A little under a minute later…

"Merchant!"

Accompanied by Ringo and Bearabbit, who'd come running over from the Manufacturing District, Tsukasa joined the group. Not even waiting to catch his breath, he immediately pressed Masato for information. The white-haired boy wanted to know if Lyrule's claim about Rage Soleil was accurate or not.

"That message you sent me, is it true?"

"…Go ahead and ask her yourself."

Tsukasa's gaze shifted to the blond girl from Elm, who was currently being tended to by Keine.

"Lyrule…do you really know how to break that spell?"

The girl nodded. Sweat was still beading on her forehead. "Rage Soleil is war magic. To cast it, you have to spend years compressing blaze spirits together. And as long as its core, the cursed spear that binds and controls the spirits, is intact, the fires will never go out! But the opposite is true, too. If you destroy the spear, you can break the spell!"

"But how do you know that…?" The question came from Akatsuki, who'd just alighted from above.

Lyrule shook her pallid head. "I…don't know…"

"You don't know?"

"I can't be sure how I know. But…even though I'm not sure why…*I know this will work!* The moment I saw those flames, I knew what kind of magic it was, what it did, everything. It all just popped into my head. It was like… It was like I'd known since before I was even born…"

"…I see."

"You probably think I'm crazy, but it's true! If we run, the fire will follow us forever! As long as that cursed core exists, it'll never stop! That's how the spell works! Please, you have to believe me!" Lyrule had no idea how she knew any of that, but even though she didn't know why, she was certain it was correct. Running away wouldn't solve anything or save anyone.

Despite realizing how unreasonable she was being, the blond girl needed to get them to understand. Lyrule had to convince the Prodigies to trust her words.

Tsukasa didn't even pause to think.

"All right. I believe you."

His reply was matter-of-fact.

"Huh…?"

"That said, the problem is how we're going to destroy the spear. That's going to be somewhat of a hurdle."

"*Yeah, all those missiles bearly scratched it. This is a toughie.*"

"Any ideas poppin' into your head about that bit, Lyrule?"

Tsukasa wasn't the only one who was immediately on board. Not a single one of the bunch cast a dubious look at Lyrule. In fact, not only were they seriously discussing the info she'd given them, they were even asking for her input.

At their unanimous response, Lyrule couldn't help but ask, "You all…really believe me…? I-it's a little strange to be saying this after I asked for your trust, but…the things I'm telling you are…crazy, aren't they?"

Tsukasa's reply was simple. "Of course we believe you." As he spoke, he pulled out a handkerchief and wiped Lyrule's cheek.

It was wet with fearful tears. Having a head full of strange information and no idea how it got there was frightening. Voices that came from nowhere were plenty startling. Indeed, it had been jarring enough to make Lyrule cry. However, that hadn't stopped the girl from speaking up.

"The change inside you was so confusing and scary, you were trembling. But you came out here to help us anyway. How could we ever doubt bravery like that?"

All the other Prodigies nodded in agreement. Seeing them treat her not with fear or revulsion but with the same trust they always did…filled Lyrule with courage.

"———!" She took a deep breath to steady her racing heart. Her body had, at last, stopped trembling. Then, in a clear, confident tone, she answered Masato's earlier question—the one about how to destroy the heart of the terrible magic.

"…Destroying the spear won't take a special power or technique. Any sort of decent blow should be able to do it."

"B-but even our missiles weren't good enough for that."

"That was before Rage Soleil activated. Back then, the spear was strong because of all the blaze spirits converged inside it… Now that Rage Soleil's activated, though, the blaze spirits have scattered throughout the city. Given its current state, an attack like one of the ones before could easily destroy it."

Hearing that, Tsukasa asked Ringo for a status report.

"Ringo, do we have any missiles left?"

"Th-there's one…loaded in Bearabbit…but…" Ringo's voice was quiet, and she curled her body up apologetically.

They did, in fact, have one missile left. It was small but designed to take out ships, so it still packed a considerable punch. Also, because it was a cruise missile, it was equipped with wings and a jet engine. Their target was well within its effective range. However, trying to hit a target as small as a spear gave rise to a new problem. Namely, how to guide the projectile.

"With how hot the flames are…guiding it…might not go too well."

Because the spear had already landed, it was outside the range of their anti-air radar. Air turbulence from the conflagration created a factor of randomness that meant guiding the missile in remotely could easily go wrong.

Compounding things was the fact that this was no ordinary fire. The way it was able to act autonomously made it more like a monster.

Masato offered a suggestion: "Couldn't Bearabbit just carry the missile in directly?"

However…

"N-no way. At the end of the day, this body is only koalafied to help Ringo with her day-to-day tasks. If I tried to go somewhere that unbearably hot, all my circuit boards would melt…"

Bearabbit shot his idea down, alarmed at the very notion. It sounded like using the missile to destroy the spear was a nonstarter.

But just as everyone was ready to give up—

*　　*　　*

"I shall go."

—Aoi Ichijou, who'd been listening silently to the discussion up until that point, announced her candidacy.

"Whaddaya mean, you'll go?"

"Once Bearabbit launches the missile, I shall run alongside it and guide it to its destination, that I shall."

""Whaaaaaaaat?!""

"I have to say, that sounds…incredibly reckless."

A human directly guiding the missile. Masato and Akatsuki reacted to the bizarre idea with outright shock, and Tsukasa laid out his entirely natural misgivings. Aoi made no effort to conceal how disappointed she was in the white-haired boy.

"Tsukasa, m'lord, with all due respect…*I ask that you not make light of me.*"

"…!"

"I am hailed the world over as a martial prodigy, that I am. My abilities lie outside your capacity to measure, and my limits are known to none in this world but myself. Thus, if I say I am capable of something, know that it can be done, no matter how hard that may be for you to believe. Tsukasa, m'lord, I ask of you this: Do you truly think I am the sort of fool who would knowingly take on a task beyond her abilities and, in doing so, endanger her friends and allies?" Aoi spoke with an air of utmost confidence about her.

As far as Tsukasa was concerned—as far as everyone but the swordswoman who'd put the idea forward was concerned—it was difficult to imagine such a thing being possible. However, they also knew that Aoi Ichijou was not the type of girl to claim she could do something she couldn't at a time like this. As their representative, Tsukasa gave his answer.

"Very well. I have faith…in our prodigious swordmaster, Aoi Ichijou." The young prime minister resolved to bet everything on the girl's abilities. Aoi gave him an unflappable, pearly-white smile.

"I shall not let you down."

Now that they had their plan, everyone got to work.

"Roo! Prince! We need to get water from the soldiers!"

"O-okay!"

"Got it!"

"I have some dressing, if you'd like. You could use it in place of a sash," Keine offered.

"I am in your debt."

"…Taking things to extremes as ever, aren't you, Aoi?"

"Such is a swordswoman's lot, that it is." Aoi took the dressing and used it to tie up her sleeves. Then, she drew her beloved katana, Hoozukimaru, and sliced her ankle-length hakama off at the knee.

"Aoi! We've got the water!"

"Ah, many thanks! Now pour it on me, if you would!"

"Comin' right up!"

"Here you go!"

"Heave ho!"

Masato, Akatsuki, and Roo took their wooden buckets and soaked Aoi from head to toe. With any luck, it would offer her body some protection against the heat. Finally, Aoi went barefoot, casting her socks and wooden sandals aside.

"Ringo, m'lady! I am prepared, that I am!" The swordmaster dropped into a crouching start as she gave Ringo her cue. The genius inventor nodded, then sat down and tapped away at her laptop. Bearabbit sprang into motion as the commands flowed in.

First, anchor bolts shot out of the manipulators he was using as legs, fastening him to the ground. Then, his display shut down and slid into his backpack body. A red-and-white missile about as thick as a man's bicep jutted out in its place. Of all the armaments loaded inside Bearabbit, that missile was his trump card. Once it was fully in position, Bearabbit gave the signal.

"I'm teddy here, too!"

"Aoi, get that missile where it needs to go!"

"That I shall!"

With her agreement serving as their final confirmation—

"Fur in the hole!"

—Bearabbit launched the missile.

The moment he did, Aoi kicked off against the ground so hard, she shattered the stone pavement.

Then, as the flame-spewing missile tried to pass her by—

"HYAAAAAAAAAAAAAAH!!!!"

—she grabbed onto its two wings and carried it with her as she dashed into the burning High-End Residential District.

©Sacranec

Aoi started by identifying the hill road that gave her the straightest shot from the central plaza to the spear's location in the High-End Residential District's park, then charged into the flames.

It wasn't as large as the main road that divided Dormundt into four sections, but it was still a wide enough berth for three carriages to comfortably pass each other by—not narrow by any definition.

Rage Soleil's fiery spawn did not take the young woman's intrusion lying down. The flaming automatons began walking toward her, trying to grab Aoi before she could reach their core. However, their speed was nothing to write home about.

It certainly wasn't enough to catch Aoi, who was using the missile's propulsion to aid her sprint. In the blink of an eye, she was out of the central plaza and heading up the hill road.

Rows of houses flanking either side of the swordswoman had been torched all the way to their roofs by flames. Aoi pushed her way through the veritable tunnel of fire at a blistering clip. Tsukasa and the others, who were watching it all play out via the camera installed on the missile's head, were at the edge of their seats.

"That's nuts. She's actually running alongside the missile…"

"Damn, I'm impressed her legs can keep up with it. At this rate, she's gonna get there in no time." However, Masato's optimism was met with doubt.

"…Unfortunately, it doesn't look like things will go quite that smoothly." Tsukasa frowned as he studied the video feed on Ringo's laptop.

Fiery figures had shuffled out of the burning houses, filling up the street and blocking Aoi's path like a wall. Forward was no longer an option. Evidently, Aoi had foreseen the appearance of such an obstacle.

"Nyaaaah!" The Prodigy shifted her center of gravity backward with all her might, no longer running with the missile but against it. She was using her entire body to yank the missile to the side.

By that point, her feet were moving faster than the untrained eye could make out. The pavement under her feet cracked and shattered, and she dug her heels into the ground beneath it to stop the missile in midair.

Then, still grasping its wings—

"Hyuh!"

—she pulled with her left hand and pushed with her right, forcibly spinning the missile around.

"Hyah!"

By smashing her honed glutes into its backside at the same time, she was able to get it to make a sharp, ninety-degree left turn toward one of the alleyways spidering off the hill road.

"She's...incredible...!" Even Ringo, who balked at talking in front of others, couldn't help but let out a cry of amazement at the nigh superhuman feat. Everyone else watching felt the same.

"This is bad...!" All except Tsukasa, the one person who had the city's layout memorized. For some reason, his expression grew grim. It wasn't long before the others discovered why.

Aoi leaned into the gentle curve, but right when she thought she'd made it through the alley—

"...!"

—she found a thirty-foot-tall burning wall in her path.

The alley didn't lead anywhere. It was a complete dead end. To make matters worse, fire creatures began creeping toward her from all directions, boxing her into the cul-de-sac like they'd been waiting for her.

"Oh no! She's trapped!"

"Aoi...!"

As far as the swordmaster was concerned, though, the situation didn't even register as a predicament. Not seeming alarmed in the slightest, she took a deep breath as she barreled toward the wall.

Then, after digging in hard with her feet, shattering the ground, and bringing the missile to a stop—

"NOW RIIIIIIIISE!"

—she pulled with all her strength and lifted the missile's head.

By doing so, she was able to shift the missile. The young woman changed its trajectory from parallel to the ground to perpendicular. The missile shot into the sky over Dormundt's burning cityscape with Aoi in tow.

Having lost their mark, the fiery figures crashed into the cul-de-sac wall and collapsed. Even they couldn't follow her into the air. At that rate, though, the missile would just keep rising, never to find its target. That wouldn't get the job done. Thankfully, Aoi had a plan.

Once she and the missile reached a certain altitude, she lifted her body as though performing a pull-up, sandwiched the missile between her sizable breasts...and blocked its air vents. By doing so, she drastically reduced the amount of oxygen flowing through the missile's internal combustion engine.

As the engine stalled, so did the projectile itself. For an instant, it hung still in the air. In that fleeting moment, Aoi let go of the vents, grabbed the wing on top of the missile, and threw herself into the air. Then, after spinning herself around the wing like it was a high bar, she leveled a solid kick at the missile's lower half.

That caused the projectile to spin upward in a semicircle. As a natural consequence, the warhead ended up pointing down. Immediately thereafter, the newly oxygenated engine fired back up.

At the end of Aoi's trapeze-like act acrobatics, she and the missile began making their way back downward. Specifically, they were gliding straight toward the High-End Residential District's park—the spot where the spear was embedded. Aoi's dramatic shortcut had allowed her to avoid every obstacle. In less than thirty seconds, the missile was going to blow the spear to kingdom come.

But then—

"...?!"

—Aoi's expression stiffened for the first time during her plan.

Down in the burning city, she saw something strange. Fire. The enchanted blaze that burned through the High-End Residential District had been trying to engulf the neighboring Port and Residential districts in turn. Now, however, it was beginning to swirl around like a whirlpool.

Flames previously spread across the city now all came falling back and converged into a vortex. Aoi's target—Rage Soleil's core—lay at the vortex's center.

Eventually, a burning pillar rose up from within the swirling crimson and took on Gustav's form once more. The duke was seething with rage.

"I imagine you shan't let me through so easily."

"Insolent little fly...!" As the massive figure of Gustav growled at her, it swung its right arm. It dredged up burnt houses by their foundations and hurled their spent wreckages at the swordswoman.

"FALL AND PERISH!"

"Rkh!"

The debris shot at her like cannon fire. In response, Aoi unfurled her legs from around the missile and used them to catch the wind and control her flight path. She wove her way between one chunk of rubble and the next. However...

"FALL, FALL, FAAAAAAAAALL!!!!"

Enraged, Gustav's fiery form cleaved through the city and sent an overwhelming barrage of debris toward her. It quickly became a struggle just to evade at all. Worse, the density of the duke's attacks only grew as Aoi got closer. At that rate, she'd end up getting shot down before ever reaching the spear.

Aoi elected to give up on her frontal assault. After dropping the missile's altitude low enough that it was grazing the tops of the taller apartment buildings, she reached out with her right hand and grabbed a passing chimney. Her fingers left five deep gashes in the brick as she used it as an axle to make a sharp right turn. By fleeing back into an alley, the young woman was able to use it as a trench against the barrage.

"Where are you hiding, pesky fly?!?!"

Even with Aoi out of his line of sight, though, Gustav didn't let up with his onslaught. He waved his hands to and fro, hurling rubble about like a child throwing a temper tantrum. Yet, with Aoi practically scraping the ground of her alley trench, none of it came anywhere close to connecting with her.

At last, she shot out of the alley into a wide, open area. It was the hill road she'd been trying to take back at the start. The detour had been long, but the High School Prodigy finally made it. Straining her eyes, Aoi could make out a long, thin object embedded in the top of the hill. It was the spear—Rage Soleil's core.

The moment Aoi spotted it—

"Ringo, m'ladyyyyyyyyy!!!!"

—she pointed the missile's warhead at the hill's peak and shouted.

"Target locked!"

Ringo's finger raced over the keyboard as she sent the missile its command. At the same time, Aoi released the projectile and shoved it forward. It barreled toward the hilltop spear. The target was a

thousand feet out—straight ahead. Even with the random temperature variations in the air, at that range, the missile was guaranteed to
hit. This was checkmate, or so they all thought...

"NOT ON MY WAAAAATCH!!!!"

"Impawsible...?!"

""""What?!"""

The camera atop the missile showed something unbelievable. Up
until now, houses flanking the road had been engulfed in fire. Now,
though, two blazing masses had blown them completely away and
were closing in on the missile from both sides. They were Gustav's
great, fiery arms. The duke was trying to smash the missile between
his hands like one would crush a pesky mosquito.

"My whirling secret technique—Dew-Blade Breeze!"

Before the Fastidious Duke could succeed, however, a tornado-
shaped vacuum burst from Hoozukimaru, slicing off the arms of
Gustav's hellish visage while leaving the missile untouched.

"AAAAAAAAAAAAAAAARGH!!!!"

"I did tell you, that I did. If I say I can do something, then do it
I can."

The missile burst out of the spiraling slash attack and smashed
head-on into the crimson spear. An explosion rocked the air, accompanied by a violent flash...

When the dust settled, not a trace of the spear remained.

A pillar of smoke and flame billowed from the High-End Residential District's peak, and everyone gazed up at it. Masato and Akatsuki

reacted with cries of admiration at their fellow Prodigy's superhuman feat.

""Aoi, that was nuts!""

Keine, on the hand, was no stranger to sharing battlefields with the swordmaster. The doctor merely shrugged in relief. "Honestly, that girl only knows how to overdo things."

The explosion wasn't the only visible change, either.

"Impossible…! How can this beeeeee?!?!" Gustav, who had manifested as a blazing colossus, screamed as his luminous flames were scattered to the wind. The fires throughout the city responded in kind, losing their vigor and vanishing into nothingness.

"L-look! The…fires…"

"They're going out…"

"…The blaze spirits were freed from the curse," Lyrule murmured as she watched the inferno flicker and wane. The blond girl could hear their voices.

"""Thank you, miss… You saved us… Thank you all…""" The spirits were expressing their gratitude.

"They're saying that now that the cursed core is destroyed, they can stop burning the city. And…they're grateful to us."

Tsukasa seemed a little surprised. "You can talk to spirits?"

Lyrule nodded. "…I've been hearing their screams this whole time. The blaze spirits were shouting 'help us' and 'we don't want to do this.' But…now, they're okay."

"Well, that's good to hear." Tsukasa gave a long exhale, then offered the long-eared woman a handshake.

"Allow me to thank you as well, Lyrule. The only reason we were able to keep the damage to the city this minimal was because of your bravery. Thank you for that."

However, Lyrule responded to his gratitude with a mixed

expression. She seemed to be half smiling and half crying. "...But there were so many people we couldn't save."

The flames were gone, and snow was falling gently from the winter sky. Lyrule looked out at the blackened city. Dormundt's High-End Residential Area had been burned to the ground.

True, the voice in her head and her sudden onrush of knowledge had allowed them to keep the city from being destroyed in its entirety. However, the things they'd lost today were never coming back. Furthermore, it was clear the tragedy was a result of their actions.

"And this all started because of what we did."

Had they not gone to war with Findolph, this calamity could have been avoided. Knowing that tormented the blond girl. Tsukasa could see it written all over her face.

"If you're thinking this wouldn't have happened if not for us starting the war...then your regrets are misplaced." The prime minister attempted to correct Lyrule's misunderstanding.

"Huh?"

"With societal growth, this war—this People's Revolution against the feudal system—was always going to happen. Even if the battle for freedom and equality in Freyjagard hadn't started in Elm, someone somewhere else would have started it instead—and just as many lives would have been lost seeing it through. But make no mistake, it would have kept on going. Just like the revolts in our world."

What Tsukasa was saying was that such tragedies were an inevitability. After all...

"Any country willing to slaughter its own citizens has no future."

"...!"

He was right. Lyrule's regrets *were* misplaced. If anything, the blame lay with the cruel oppressors who had made the revolution a necessity in the first place.

Even if Lyrule and the others had done nothing, as long as the noble class viewed the commoners as wretched worms, horrors like this would have happened time and time again.

"In other words, we shouldn't give in to remorse and seek forgiveness from those whose lives were lost. Instead, we need to see this fight through to secure a future for the billions of lives waiting to come into this world. Don't you agree?"

"...Y-yes!" Lyrule gave Tsukasa a big nod and returned his handshake. Her grip was firm and resolute.

No sooner had she done so than—

"Hey! There they are! The God and his angels!"

"Th-that's incredible! They stayed here this whole time?!"

"They must have been the ones who took down that giant monster!"

"Thank you, God!"

—the townsfolk, seeing that the fire had gone out, streamed back into the city.

They were all wondering the same thing: Had the Seven Luminaries really defeated the creature of flame? When they saw the Prodigies standing in the central plaza, the battlefield's front line, the citizens let out a resounding cheer. Tsukasa looked out over the crowd as a tidal wave of joy washed over them all.

"Ladies and gentlemen, rejoice! God Akatsuki's miracle has obliterated the empire's monster! Not even a flaming beast that towers to the heavens poses a threat to our God!"

As the crowd's excitement swelled, the white-haired boy clapped Akatsuki on the shoulder.

"They're all warmed up for you. Go get 'em."

"Wait, you're getting them riled up and then bailing on me?"

"I have a postmortem with the mayor I need to get to. Sorry, but I'm delegating this one to you." Tsukasa scurried away from Akatsuki to make his escape.

As he tried to leave, though—

"Tsukasa!"

—Lyrule called out to him. With a serious look on her face, she told him about the woman who'd spoken to her in her dream.

"Right before this all started, I heard a voice in my dream. A woman told me that I needed to use my power to guide the Seven Heroes."

"Oh?" Tsukasa stopped in his tracks and looked back over his shoulder.

"Then, right after she spoke to me, knowledge about magic started welling up in my mind and I was able to hear the spirits."

"The timing seems too serendipitous to write it off as merely an odd dream."

"Isn't it? I have no idea who it was or why I could hear her, but... when she said 'my power,' I think she was talking about my knowledge of magic and my ability to hear spirits. So..." Lyrule paused for a moment and took a deep breath to steel herself before resuming.

"...I'm going to start studying magic! Once I can use it, I might be able to help you fight, and also...if this person talking to me has something to do with why you seven are here in this world, I might be able to help you all find a way back home...!" Lyrule's eyes burned bright with the light of fresh determination.

Tsukasa could tell that resolve of hers was going to be a big asset for him and his friends. The young man's lips curled into a soft smile as he spoke. "...Honestly, that would be fantastic. I've actually picked up quite a bit about magic over this past month myself, so if you need any help, don't hesitate to ask."

At the same time, back in Gustav's castle, the duke himself was howling in agony.

"AAAAAAAAAAAAAAAARGH!!!!"

"M-milord?!" Hearing the screams, Oscar came running, but what he found shocked him. Both of the Fastidious Duke's arms had been severed from the elbow down.

"Milord, are you all right?! What happened…?!"

However, it was like Gustav didn't even hear him. The man merely stared at the blood gushing from his stumps in disbelief.

"H-how can this be…?! My Rage Soleil…was destroyed?!" There was a quiver in the man's voice.

Through Rage Soleil, he'd been able to witness everything that had transpired in Dormundt. Of note, he'd seen Aoi dodging his attacks as she carried her missile.

Those garments, that sword… She's a Yamato agent, I'm sure of it!

But that missile, the flame-spitting, free-flying cannonball? It was the first time he'd seen anything like it. Gustav had no idea what to make of it. Who were those people? Clearly, they couldn't have been mere survivors from Yamato. For whatever reason, the northern rebellion had access to weapons that even the Yamato Imperial Army hadn't. But why?

Gustav had no idea.

There was one thing he was certain of, however. Those scuttling little things were no ordinary pests. They were a threat—not just to the north, but to the entire empire, and even to Emperor Lindworm.

"…!" The duke could not tolerate their continued existence, not for another minute, not for another second!

At the moment, Emperor Lindworm was off in the New World. What kind of knight would Gustav be if he failed to protect the realm in his master's absence?! Was that conduct befitting a noble?!

"RrrrrrrRRRRRGRRRAAAAHHH!!!!"

After cauterizing his wounds with magic fire, arms of crimson flames sprouting from his stumps, Gustav rose.

"Oscaaaar…"

The duke's eyes burned with rage as he looked down upon his aide.

"Y-yes, milord?!"

"Summon every soldier in the domain to the capital at once. The full might of our forces will march on Findolph!"

"B-but didn't you delegate that to Marquis Archride?"

"That dithering incompetent allowed vermin to fester in His Grace's sacred lands for over a month! He's useless to me!

"Relay this to those fools Archride and Buchwald: We leave not a single ant alive in our wake! And unless they do their damned jobs and march, they, too, will find themselves tasting the flames of my wrath!"

❦ A Battle Ignited ❦

It was just before dawn. The snow had stopped falling, but it was still bitter cold outside. Over in a nook of the High-End Residential District's park, a trio of former nobles shivered as they stared at the burnt remains of their homes.

"What's...what's gonna happen to us?"

"Hell if I know."

The pudgy youth sounded like he was on the verge of tears, but Kyle, their *byuma* leader, replied bluntly.

"I had no idea the empire would take such extreme measures while we nobles were still in the city..." The tall youth, who'd lost his glasses in the evacuation, seemed to be at his wit's end. As a relative of Marquis Archride's, the young man had never felt so fearful for his life before. However, the truth laid out before their eyes was all too clear. They'd been left with nothing.

But as they crouched there despondently—

"Hey, wee nobles over there."

—a middle-aged common-born woman holding a stack of blankets called out to them.

"We've got a fire goin' and some food cookin', so c'mon over. And here, take these. You kids'll catch your death of cold, dressed as you are." The woman handed them each one of the quilts. Two of them eagerly received the kindness, but Kyle...

"...Giving charity to nobles, huh? I bet you're getting a real kick outta this." Still crouching, he glared at her and spat out a snide remark.

"Wh—?!"

"K-Kyle, this is no time to be saying stuff like that...!"

"Y-yeah, that's right! C'mon, you gotta apologize...!"

The *byuma* was uninterested in the advice of his friends, however. His upbringing and the way he'd lived his life forbade him from accepting anything from the woman. Why should a noble like him have to accept charity from a commoner? He would've rather frozen to death than live with the shame.

Instead of reaching out, he piled on the vitriol.

"You rabble must be having a hoot seeing us like this. You're all filthy hypocrites!"

The woman sighed in exasperation. "Look, you nobles spent generations actin' all high and mighty and lookin' down on us even though you didn't do squat. If you ask me if I like y'all or not, to be honest, I hate your guts." The woman gazed down at Kyle with contempt in her eyes.

"See?! Then why even bother?" But when Kyle tried to shoo her away...

"But noble or commoner, an empty belly on a cold winter night hurts just the same."

Suddenly, warmth filled the young *byuma* boy's body. The woman had draped the blanket around his shivering shoulders. As she stared straight into his bloodshot eyes, the corners of her mouth curled into a gentle smile.

"We're all just people, and we know darn well how tough life can be. We're not about to leave you boys in the lurch."

"Rkh…!"

"Now, c'mon and get your butts over here already. Gimme any more lip, and I'll just drag you there myself!"

With that, the woman hoisted Kyle up by the collar and carted him off. As an aristocrat, he'd never worked a day in his life. To him, this older woman seemed unbelievably strong. Her actions left Kyle at a loss for words.

He couldn't bring himself to spew any more complaints or hostility. That smile she'd given him had begun melting the cold around his heart. In that moment, Kyle finally realized something—just how little he understood. The pompous *byuma* had known nothing about the world or the kindness of the people who lived in it. Such a realization brought a tremble to his voice.

"…I'm sorry…"

In his heart, Kyle resolved to confess to the Seven Luminaries about the terrorist attack he'd been plotting with the Roaring Thunder bombs.

Meanwhile, Tsukasa Mikogami was sitting atop the burnt wreckage of the city's municipal office and talking to someone on the phone. The call was from Shinobu Sarutobi, who was in the middle of her mission to infiltrate the Gustav domain.

After getting in touch with the Blue Brigade resistance movement, she'd heard about Heavenly Fire—the war magic known as Rage Soleil—and had retrieved her phone from Elch to warn Tsukasa of its danger.

However, upon discovering her report had come too late—

*   *   *

"NO WAAAAAAAAAAAAAAAAAAAAAAAY!!!!"

—she shrieked so loudly the phone speaker's audio peaked.

Tsukasa's right ear took the hit directly, very nearly blowing out his eardrum. With a grimace, the boy switched the phone to his still-functioning left ear and made his displeasure known.

"Keep it down, Shinobu."

"So wait, you're serious? You guys already got hit by Rage Soleil?!"

"Indeed."

"I-is everyone okay?! From what I heard, that spell is a real nasty piece of work!"

"Everyone pulled together, so we were able to limit the damages to only a third of the city."

"Oof... Th-this is a bad look. In fact, if I had to rank every humiliating thing that's ever happened to me, this'd be third from the top! I'm supposed to always get the scoop on dirty dealings before they go live, but this time, I missed my deadline! I mean, Gustav did go off on his own without even getting in touch with his army... Dammit. Has this guy never heard of a little thing called patience?! Go bald, jackass!"

"If it's all the same to you, I'd rather you keep the strange curses to yourself."

Shinobu, who normally hid her true feelings behind an evasive front, was throwing a fit like a child. She must really have been upset. After all, the prodigy journalist prided herself on being the best. Finding that fact somewhat reassuring, Tsukasa changed the subject.

"...As far as Rage Soleil goes, what's done is done. There's no point brooding about it. Now, about this resistance you mentioned...the Blue Brigade. Good work getting in contact with them. That alone made your mission well worth the effort. I want you and Elch to continue working with them while feeding us any strategic information they give you. I'll need intel on those rebels, too... There's no guarantee they'll stay an ally forever."

"*...Aight, got it. I'll text you what I know so far.*"

"Please do."

"*I really am sorry, you know...*"

After an apology that sounded like she was on the verge of tears, the call ended. Masato, who'd been waiting in the wings with a stack of papers in one hand, called over to Tsukasa.

"Was that Shinobu?"

"It was. She was calling to warn us about Rage Soleil."

"Little late to the party on that one."

"And quite torn up about it, too."

"Ha-ha. Yeah, that's gotta be a rough blow for a top journalist like her," Masato laughed. "But hey, these things happen, y'know?" The fact that Shinobu regularly exposed the Sanada Group's legally murky dealings probably factored into Masato's amusement.

"Oh, and by the way, what was that 'last idea' of yours?"

"Hmm? What are you talking about?"

"When you called us, you said you might have a way to deal with the magic fire, remember?"

"Ah, that," Tsukasa replied. "It was more or less the same as what Lyrule told us. I was going to suggest firing another missile at the spear. Apparently, magic's power is proportional to the number of spirits it employs. The more ice spirits your ice bullet uses, the greater its penetrative power; the more wind spirits you use in your wind slash, the sharper it'll be.

"With enough of them, even mere spears of frozen water made with tactical magic could pierce iron shields. Taking that into account, converged-state war magic is probably tougher than steel. It made sense that our missiles couldn't break it...but with the flames spread out around the city, I thought we might have a chance. It was all just conjecture, though; no guarantee it would've worked."

"Yeah, but you hit the nail on the head."

"In this world, magic is just another technical system. Proper research goes a long way. I took what I'd learned and made an educated guess."

After making it all sound easy, Tsukasa picked up his phone to make another call. Seeing his friend like that filled Masato with confidence. Magic hadn't even existed in their world, but in just one short month, Tsukasa had been able to get enough of a grasp on it to make an accurate prediction in a time of crisis.

Lyrule's awakening had been an unexpected boon for them, but even without that, Tsukasa had already taken the threat magic posed into account and made proper preparations to deal with it. Honestly, the guy was unreal.

Y'know, you're the only person in this whole world I can truly rely on. That was precisely what made Tsukasa so scary.

You're trying to save as many people as you can, and I'm trying to get my hands on as much stuff as I can. Eventually...our paths are gonna diverge.

Masato was certain of it. At some point, he and his childhood friend were going to end up as enemies. That battle was bound to be the fiercest, most trying battle the Devil of Finance would ever face. A pang of loneliness crossed Masato's face as he thought about the future.

"Oh, Merchant, there was something I wanted to tell you. Lyrule remembered something." Tsukasa was evidently finished with his short conversation.

"Apparently, she heard a female voice in her dream telling her that she needed to 'guide the Seven Heroes.'"

Burying his worries for the future, Masato replied, "Huh... That's pretty specific, isn't it?"

"I'd suspected as much since the incident at Castle Findolph, but Lyrule, the reason we're here, and this strange woman's voice all seem deeply connected. The voice wants us to defeat this 'evil dragon' or what have you, and it also wants Lyrule to help us do it... Given the information we have so far, that's about the shape of things."

"Well, at least this voice doesn't seem like an enemy..."

"...But there's no guarantee it's an ally, either."

"True, true. Hey, you said you were looking into Lyrule's origins, right? How'd that go?"

"I stopped by Elm last week and asked Winona and the mayor about it again. Nothing new on that front."

"They just found her in the woods, huh?"

Tsukasa nodded.

"I kept an eye on their pupils and lip movements, but it didn't seem as though either of them was lying."

"So we're at an impasse..."

"It's fine. This time, the unknown took a step toward us. Besides, once we decided that we'd see the People's Revolution through, information on how to get home shifted down in our priority list. Right now, what we should be worrying about...is what's listed in that stack of papers you're holding."

"You can say that again." The prodigy businessman heaved a gloomy sigh as he rapidly flipped through the stack. That was all he needed to parse the words and numbers recorded within. Enumerated on the documents was a list of all the food and supplies that Dormundt had lost in the fire.

"Thanks to those inventories you had us put together in advance, rebuilding the city should go pretty smoothly, but the food situation's a little dire. Losing the Port District's warehouses hit us pretty hard."

"How long do we have?"

"Even with contributions from nearby villages, we're gonna run dry in about a month... And that's right when winter gets its coldest and nastiest."

"I figured as much."

"Yep. So what's the plan?"

"This." As the word left Tsukasa's mouth, a throng of soldiers came rushing over and stood at attention before them. At their head was the Order of the Seven Luminaries' commander, Bernard. His voice boomed as he spoke.

"Mr. Tsukasa, the first squadron's armaments have been fully modernized. We're fifty in total, at your call."

It was just as the commander said. The soldiers had traded their armor for winter gear and their swords and spears for the newly minted wood-and-iron firearms.

In the Le Luk Mountain Range, it was a struggle just finding somewhere to stand. However, there was a single, wide, smooth road that cut across that treacherous terrain.

A few generations ago, when the Freyjagard Empire had ordered the Findolph family to break ground to the north, they'd carved their way through the mountains and built the mountainous region's only road capable of supporting carriage traffic.

Naturally, such a path had a checkpoint.

The stone brickwork checkpoint barred the way to the mountain's wide valley, and it boasted a gigantic gate easily thirty feet tall.

Normally, it had fifty Buchwald soldiers stationed in it, keeping watch twenty-four hours a day. Now that they were on high alert, though, that number had been quadrupled. The checkpoint stood two hundred guardsmen strong. They were split into three teams, each taking an eight-hour shift, and together, they made sure to survey from every direction.

It was midnight, a few days after Rage Soleil had set Dormundt on fire.

"Gah, I'm freezing my balls off here. Looks like we've got another blizzard today, too."

"Hey, it's time for the shift change."

"Ah, you're a lifesaver. If I had to stay in this drafty rat trap any longer, I'd probably freeze to death."

"Yeah, they could at least put up some glass windows or something."

There were a number of little watchhouses mounted atop the stone ramparts stretching across the mountain valley. The soldiers stationed in one of them glanced off into the blizzard as they shivered from the bone-chilling cold.

"Nah, glass'd get all fogged up. Can't keep watch if you can't see."

"Who cares? Not like anyone'd be stupid enough to try crossing Le Luk in the winter... Now, c'mon, let's get back to the barracks already. I wanna sneak some booze and jerky from the larders on our way back."

Hearing the gaunt-faced soldier say that took his stubbly, stern-looking partner aback. "Hey, whoa, they execute people for that kind of stuff."

"Not if they don't find out. The cold storage is always packed to the gills during the winter, and with how they're prepping for war this year, it's practically overflowing. Who's gonna notice if a bottle or two goes missing?"

"Yeah, I say go for it. The battalion commander turns a blind eye to that stuff on purpose. After all, going to sleep in weather like this without a little something to warm you up means you risk not waking up at all."

Seeing the relief-shift soldiers agree so strongly turned the sterner guardsman's opinion around. "Well, when you put it like that…"

"Then hey, let's—"

But right as the two off-the-clock watchmen made to leave their post, something unusual happened.

The sound of an explosion rocked the ears of the four guards, and a mighty tremor ran through the floor.

"Wh-what's going on?!"

After frantically grabbing torches, they made for the ramparts and looked down. The soldiers stationed at the next watchhouse over looked to be doing the same. Below, they spotted it: a massive hole blown in the side of the wall's masonry.

"Th-there's a hole in the wall?!"

"If someone broke through, d-does that mean the noise just now was cannon fire?!"

From atop the ramparts, the soldiers squinted in disbelief out into the thick darkness. That very same moment, a number of sparks flashed in the rumbling gloom.

"Gah?!"

A few soldiers toppled backward, blood gushing from their bodies.

"Was that gunfire just now?!"

"Th-there's no way! No one could aim a gun in a blizzard like—geh!"

"No, it is; I'm positive! We're under fire!"

Bullets were barreling out of the blackness, speeding toward the soldiers visible atop the ramparts. At that point, there was no doubting it. One of the soldiers let out the cry of alarm.

"We're under attaaaaaaack!"

* * *

No sooner had he done so than the alarm bells affixed to the watchhouses all began sounding, and the checkpoint came alive. The guardsmen had already been on high alert, so a squad of crossbow archers was ready on the wall in no time.

However...

"Agh!"

"Gah?!"

"What are you doing?! Hurry up and return fire!"

"We can't, Captain! I-it's too dark to see, so we don't know where to shoo—geh?!"

"Rgh...!"

The lack of light and the raging blizzard meant the soldiers had no recourse against the unbelievably accurate bullets but to roll over and die. The resident Bronze Knight captain had no idea what to make of it.

The only guns the man could think of capable of shooting accurately in a snowstorm were flintlock rifles. However, those were so new that even the forces in the imperial capital weren't all equipped with them yet. Most of the Freyjagard Army was still using matchlock guns.

What's more, defending Findolph hadn't exactly been high on the empire's list of priorities. As far as the knight knew, the region barely had any guns at all. How had the rebels who'd overthrown Findolph gotten their hands on such quality armaments? Perhaps more importantly, even if the insurgents did have flintlock rifles...

"How are they shooting us so accurately when it's this pitch dark...?!"

The answer to that question lay on the heads of the Order of the Seven Luminaries' fifty-man squad. Each one of them was wearing a large pair of goggles. The genius inventor, Ringo Oohoshi, had armed the battalion with night-vision specs.

"These are great! Still wish we had some sunlight, but even with how dark it is, I can totally make the enemies out!"

"The guns are nasty, too. Wind's completely nuts, but most of our shots are still landing. This magic gear from the angels is no joke!"

It wasn't exactly magic, but there was still a good reason for the strength of the weapons. Their guns, produced at the arms factory beside the power plant in Dormundt, made use of a technique that even the imperial workshops hadn't been able to come up with a cost-efficient way of implementing. It was a process called broaching—in short, they had rifling. Older gun models couldn't hold a candle to them when it came to range and ballistic stability.

All fifty of the soldiers from Dormundt were equipped with night-vision goggles and rifles, making their ranged battle against the hundred-odd crossbow archers decidedly one-sided. Little by little, the Order of the Seven Luminaries whittled down their enemy's ranks while the Buchwald army remained unable to land a single bolt. Eventually, the imperial side seemed to have their hands full reloading, as their crossbow fire died down for a moment.

Now's the time!

Commander Bernard used that pause to give his order. "Conrad Squadron! Concentrate your fire on the top of the fortress wall! Don't let them stick their heads out!"

""""Yes, sir!"""""

"Bernard Squadron, you're with me! Charge!"

""""Hraaaaaaah!"""""

At the command, twenty or so soldiers who'd been chosen in advance roared as they charged through the snow toward the checkpoint's bastion.

"A battle cry?!"

"This is bad! They're rushing toward that hole they blew open!"

"Don't let them inside! Shoot to kill!"

Having finished reloading their crossbows, the soldiers obeyed their captain and leaned out over the ramparts to take aim at the now-visible insurgents.

As brave as a frontal charge may have seemed, the snow was up to the incursion's calves. Getting anywhere fast was out of the question. Even through a blizzard, they were like sitting ducks.

However—

"Damn th—akh?!"

—a fierce barrage of gunfire hammered the ramparts and stopped the archers in their tracks. Two storms surged through the mountain pass now, and one was made of lead.

"I-it's no use! There's too much gunfire for us to risk sticking our heads out!"

"There's too many of them! They'll blow us away the second we stand!"

"Rgh…!"

The Bronze Knight captain couldn't even rebuke what his men were saying. He himself was thinking the very same thing. The leaden squall pounded over their heads without letting up for a moment.

To the warriors of this world, who were only familiar with guns that required manual reloading from the muzzle after every shot, the rapid-fire barrage was like a bolt-action nightmare. The hearts of the guardsmen froze over, and it had nothing to do with the temperature. The ability to maintain that level of high-density fire was unbelievable.

Just how many hundreds of flintlock snipers does the enemy have out there?!

It had been a short while now since the battle started over on the Findolph side of the checkpoint.

From the Buchwald side, the back door attached to the main gate swung open, and five soldiers waded into the snow. Each was a messenger tasked with delivering news of the enemy raid to the main army down in the foothills.

With desperate expressions on their faces, the quintet rushed through the snow. Each was eager to escape the hellish site of battle as quickly as possible. Then, right as the sounds of the insurgents' gunfire began to fade into the distance...

"Ah—"

"Huh?"

Bang, bang, bang.

Sparks flashed from the dark nearby, and all five couriers crumpled onto the ground. A little while afterward, five figures robed in white cloth crunched across the snow.

"...I won't apologize for this. Our lives are on the line just as much as yours were." The voice speaking to the dead men was dignified, despite its obvious youth. It belonged to Tsukasa Mikogami. In order to cut off any messengers the checkpoint might've sent, the young prime minister had led a small group around to its Buchwald side.

"Still, these Le Luk bastards are all sorts of shoddy."

"Yeah, for real. We managed to sneak past their defenses like they were nothing."

"Maybe they're all just napping on the job 'cause it's too cold."

The exasperation of the Seven Luminaries' soldiers was only natural. After all, they hadn't needed to hide, take a treacherous route, or anything of the like.

They just strolled across the mountain.

By doing so, they'd found themselves on the other side of the checkpoint in no time at all. Such an achievement brought on a wave of relief for the soldiers. Perhaps their enemies weren't as tough as they'd been made out to be. However, Tsukasa knew that wasn't the case.

His group not getting caught had nothing to do with the Buchwald army's proficiency. The thing was, the route they'd taken was the same path Shinobu and Elch had used to cross the border themselves. If anything, Shinobu's ability to spot the holes in defenses was just that fearsome. Little of the merit for their feat belonged to the young white-haired man and his soldiers.

Tsukasa barked an order to the others to keep them from letting their guards down. "That's enough chatter. Our job is to stay here until the Bernard Squadron conquers the checkpoint, shooting any enemies who try to flee. We can't let a single person through. If anyone escapes, *it's game over.* Keep your wits about you."

""""Y-yes, sir.""""

The four soldiers obediently straightened up. It was clear from their conduct how much they respected the boy with heterochromatic eyes.

The angels of the Seven Luminaries had built weapons these troops had never seen before, improved conditions for the common folk, and even defeated a giant fire monster. After they'd accomplished all that, there were none left who doubted their divinity.

Meanwhile, as Tsukasa and his men were cutting off their enemies' escape route from the Buchwald side...

Bernard's squadron had taken the western half of the east-west bifurcated checkpoint. They raced through the central courtyard, ready to claim the opposite side as well.

"D-dammit! How'd they get this far already?!"

"The west side is done for! Lower the iron gate!"

Unable to fight back against the power of modern weaponry, the checkpoint's guards fled to the east half. Despite the fact that they still had allies stuck on the west side, the retreating men dropped a heavy iron grille onto the path that led out from the central courtyard.

"H-hey! You're just gonna leave us here?!"

"You bastaaaaards!"

"Commander, there's an iron gate…!"

"Leave it to me."

Bernard took a step forward and readied his weapon.

The gun, which consisted of a short, squat barrel affixed to a disk, hadn't been built in the arms factory. It was a special weapon Bear-abbit had made himself, and the AI only gave it to those he trusted—a grenade launcher.

The explosive Bernard fired hit the grille with a peculiar *plink*, then detonated in a large explosion.

Just like the checkpoint's outer wall before it, the gate was completely blasted away—along with the enemy soldiers who'd been clinging to it.

"…M-magic…?" One soldier who'd miraculously survived let out a small yelp as he stared, aghast, at the obliterated barricade.

Bernard and his men rushed past the frightened survivor, charging into the east wing. Their enemies were forced farther and farther up and responded to the insurgent push by forming a defensive line on the east wing's spiral staircase.

The corkscrew set of stairs had been built counterclockwise on purpose. That way, intruders coming from below wouldn't be able to use their dominant hands, whereas the defenders above would have no such restriction.

However—

"Don't retreat this far, idiots! You're practically handing them the fort on a silver platter!"

"E-easy for you to say…!"

"What's with their shields?! They're so huge, but they're carrying them like they weigh nothing!"

—even that was no match for the duralumin shields the intruders' vanguard was carrying.

Spears, clubs, and swords were all rendered useless. The silvery shields repelled them all and forced the Buchwald soldiers to give more and more ground.

Finally, their brawny Bronze Knight leader roared in exasperation, "All right, rank and file, outta the way! I, Bronze Knight Gambino the Great, will take them on myself!"

He kicked his allies aside, then swung his metal flail toward the duralumin shields. The weapon's iron ball weighed over forty pounds, meaning it should have easily crushed the shields and skulls of the invaders in one fell swing.

However—

"_____"

—it was like they'd known it was coming, as a double-barreled shotgun peeked its head out from the gap between two shields.

Fire erupted.

Bronze Knight Gambino, who'd made a valiant charge on his foes, felt a terrible impact in his abdomen. Blown against the stairs, he passed out. The shot had left a gruesome dent in the man's armor.

Instead of lead, the shotgun was packed with buckshot made from small stones. At close range, the attack had quite literally rocked him. The Bronze Knight was going to be out for a while, and with no CO, the Buchwald soldiers were routed.

"Eeeeeeek?!?!"

"Ah! They got Gambino the Great!"

"We can't stop them! No one can stop them!"

The guardsmen grew more and more terrified by the minute. As far as they were concerned, power that overwhelming could've only been magic. Against such strength, all they could do was scream and flee.

"Their weapons are nuts! Who are these people?!"

Well, that and curse their misfortune for having been there in the first place.

An hour after the battle started, Tsukasa got a call from Bernard. It was to inform the young politician that they'd seized complete control of the checkpoint. When he heard the news, Tsukasa turned around, looked toward the Buchwald side of the fortress, and thought back.

The boy recalled the conversation he'd had with Masato in front of the soldiers before they'd launched the attack.

"...Hey, yo, what's the plan here?"

While Masato glanced at the fully armed soldiers, Tsukasa had answered.

"As I'm sure a tremendous businessman like yourself is well aware, patience is an indispensable quality for anyone hoping to manage personnel or capital.

"Gustav is the type of man to fire off his Rage Soleil without waiting to mobilize an army. The odds that he keeps himself in check until the snow melts are slim. In fact, I imagine he's already getting ready to march on us. And he's probably given Buchwald's and Archride's forces the order to move out, as well. I'd bet the duke told them that he'd cut them down from behind if anyone questioned his order. With the Warden of the North being so forceful, they had no choice but to follow his command.

"However, they prepared all their equipment under the assumption the invasion would be in spring. Crossing Le Luk in the gear they have *will be a suicide march; it's the best chance we could have asked for. I see no reason to sit around waiting for them to cross the range. Do you?"*

Tsukasa's tone had been matter-of-fact, but a cruel, fierce light had burned in his blue eye.

"We'll meet them in the mountains, slaughter them, and take the three northern domains before winter's end. With that territory in hand, we'll raise the flag of our democratic nation."

It was thus that a new battle began.

AFTERWORD

Happy New Year!

I'm Riku Misora, the author.

This is my first book of 2016, so even though it's February already, I wanted to give you all a New Year's greeting. In my defense, I'm technically writing this in the middle of January, so I hope you'll cut me some slack :P

By the way, I'd like to thank you all for last year. I mentioned this on the book's belly band as well, but you helped *High School Prodigies Have It Easy Even in Another World!* get off to an amazing start.

I'll try to make the rest of the series good enough to be worthy of the overwhelming support you've shown. I hope you'll all continue reading it.

Next, I'd like to thank everyone for reading the second volume of *High School Prodigies Have It Easy Even in Another World!* (*Choyoyu* for short, a nickname that comes from the Japanese title) through to the end.

In Volume 2, Akatsuki used his "miracles" (illusions) to build a military through religious support.

Then, Ringo got a stable source of fuel to support her present-day-level factory and was able to modernize part of their army. Compared to Volume 1, where her main trick was the duralumin, she was able to strengthen their faction a great deal.

Also, Shinobu sneaked deep into enemy territory; Aoi and the awakened Lyrule were able to ward off Gustav's supposed trump card, Rage Soleil; and the High School Prodigies managed to steadily back him—a commander of the empire—into a corner. However, only time will tell if they manage to make good on Tsukasa's claim, beat Gustav, and take the three northern domains before winter's end.

I hope you all continue watching over the High School Prodigies as they make their way through their new world in the next volume and beyond.

Now, I'd like to hijack this space for a bit and thank all the people who put their hard work into *Choyoyu*'s second volume.

Sacraneco, thank you for all your delightful illustrations! When I hit my Volume 2 *kunoichi* quota by having Shinobu get captured by the enemy, I thought, *I gotta see this part illustrated!* When I saw the art, I was beside myself with joy!

I'd also like to thank my editor, Kohara, and the rest of the editorial staff over at GA Bunko. Having you all point out my typos and omitted words was a huge help.

Finally, my utmost gratitude to all the readers who stuck with me for not just one but two whole volumes.

I'll do my best to repay you all in the form of interesting stories!

Anyway, that's all from me! I hope we meet again in book three!

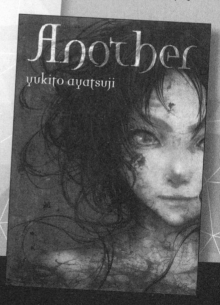